TAPS

SIXTY BEATS PER MINUTE.
THE MEASURE OF A LIFE.

Kenn Borden

This is a work of fiction. Any characters, businesses,
places, events, and incidents are either the products
of the author's imagination or used in a fictitious
manner. Any resemblance to actual persons, living
or dead, or actual events is purely coincidental.

Printed in the United States of America

ISBN: 978-1-953910-63-9 (paperback)
ISBN: 978-1-953910-64-6 (ebook)

Canoe Tree
Press

4697 Main Street
Manchester Center, VT 05255

Canoe Tree Press is a division of DartFrog Books.

DEDICATION

To Tamara, Darcy, and Jeffrey
Three who have been there for me,
And to Keith, one who could not...

Contents

1 | Frankenshoes 9
2 | The Promised Land 23
3 | Brocco-Roni & Cheese 43
4 | Arrythmia 63
5 | To Be Mediocre 77
6 | Sproingy-Thingy 91
7 | Of Oboes and Ogres 109
8 | Route 7-B 123
9 | To the Heart 139
10 | What If? 149
11 | Smyrnaean Blood 159
12 | Spectacles 171
13 | Parradiddles 179
14 | Tastee-Freeze 191
15 | The Eric 205
16 | Again? 215
17 | Taps 223
Acknowledgements 237
About the Author 239

"Some people are more talented than others. Some are more educationally privileged than others, but we all have the capacity to be great. Greatness comes by recognizing your potential is limited by how you choose, how you use your freedom, how resolute you are. Greatness comes by your attitude. We are all free to choose our attitude."
—Pete Koestenbaum

1 \ FRANKENSHOES

THE BOY'S HEART RACED in apprehension. Again. The choice had already been made for him. Again. He looked to his feet, sighed, and placed one gigantic Frankenshoe in front of the other. He slowly began to climb a mountain of steps.

"Pick up your feet!" commanded his mother, already and always at least three steps ahead—never on his side. "Come on, you're already late for school!"

"I'm late?" The boy's words were inner screams, but outwardly they were barely a mumble. He didn't look up. He didn't look at his mother. The cold, dreary, overcast, November day matched the young boy's soul. This would be his third try at a new high school in as many months. He was in ninth grade, when they were not moving, and it seemed like they were always moving. At least he was not failing; that would be against the laws of all his up bringing.

His mother, Mrs. Addison Schyler, was a stickler for perfection; her standards for herself (and especially for others, the boy thought), were exceedingly high. Mrs. Schyler was tall at five feet, seven inches, and still slim for forty-three. To keep her figure, she ate little and exercised much, often having the boy join her. He felt embarrassed by this; he would grumble, but to no avail. Usually, grumbling meant more sit ups. She would hold his ankles; he would have to do the same for her.

Her dress was always immaculate, no jeans for her, no yoga pants (unless doing yoga, of course!). Usually, it was a dress and heels, "proper," she would say. She did not leave the house without every seam ironed and every curl of her dark brown, Clairol-assisted, hair in place. She would not allow herself to be viewed as unprepared or unkempt. She was perfect in mannerisms, bound by pleases and thank yous, and she demanded respect from all. This went as far as the boy's title for her: never Mom, only Mother.

Neither would she allow her offspring to draw unwanted attention. It was *her* twenty minutes of extra pre-school preening, and *her* discussion about behaviors, that had made him late for his first day. Addison's instructions had been crystal clear. "You will not disrespect your teachers. You will listen, take notes, and study. We will not do again what we just got away from in Tennessee. You embarrassed me, and you should be ashamed of yourself. We are here to start over."

"I'm late?" The angry boy dared to raise his voice. She was farther still up the never-ending staircase, and she would not hear. The boy often talked to himself. He felt he had no one else. *I'm late?* He kicked the side of the step. *You're driving.* Kick. *Your choice of school.* Kick. *Your decision to move again!* Kick! *Your G— D— Frankenshoes!* He would not cuss. It was improper.

Rage pulsed through his body with each beat against the concrete. He stopped, keeping his eyes firmly directed toward his shoes. He was stalling. He bent his already oversized five-foot, eleven-inch frame. His dad had been six foot four, so he still had a way to go. He struggled to keep his balance on spindly legs, as he played at tying his shoes. His brown hair, the same color as his mother's—and needing to be cut, she would tell him—fell into his brown eyes—the same color as his mothers. *I am her!*

He despised his Frankenshoes. No Nike or Converse for him. The massive shoes were Walmart specials: size 13, black, shiny, leather, dress shoes. These were shoes that had to be polished! To the boy, they were combat boots.

Mother had picked them out. "They'll make you look professional, studious. Clothes make the man! You'll stick out as someone who cares about learning, someone who wants to know," she had said, as she walked away. "Now let's go find you some dress pants."

I'll stick out alright! At fourteen, showing up at another new school just two days before Thanksgiving break while wearing new, shiny shoes, and new, shiny pants, and growing inches per day, he was floundering in thoughts of gangly and awkward. He was always noticed for the wrong things and never for the right. He slowly retied the second shoe.

His mother was almost to the top of the staircase, so he risked speaking louder. "I'll stick out alright!" He stood up, pushing his dark-rimmed and thick-lensed glasses back up his nose. He had absolutely no interest in using them to view what was ahead of him; he already knew. Kids would laugh. They always laugh. But there was no way to escape the intensity of the spotlight, focused on him by his mother's need for him to be above the rest. He was a forced schoolkid. "You are 'smarter than the average bear,'" she would say, referencing some long-forgotten cartoon character. *Am I? How will I ever know?*

"Criminy!" he spoke aloud. "Why'd you have to park so far away?"

She would not, could not, hear him.

He took another few steps, desperately scuffing his Frankenshoes as he went. His head ached in singsong: *Meet the new school, same as the old school; meet the new teachers, same as the old teachers; meet the new friends...* Well, that would not change, he had never had the chance to create any of those anywhere.

The steps plateaued, and the reluctant student reached the open door. His mother held it for him; her face shown proudly upon him. "See, I knew you could do it!" As if he was two and had just learned how to pee in the toilet and not in his diaper. He didn't look at her. He was uninterested even in the name of the school, chiseled in large letters on the front of an old, crumbly, brick building. *Meet the new school...*

Inside, a round and uniformed security guard, whose name tag identified him as Mr. Escobar, slouched in front of a long, tall counter. He stood and planted his hand on his gun as if in warning, but his voice was friendly enough, "Hi, young man," he said.

The boy glanced up long enough to see the man smile at him and dip his head to the boy's mother. The boy forced a nod.

Seated behind the counter was a tired-looking woman. She stood, smiled as if it was a duty, and reached out her hand to the boy and his mother. "Hello. I'm Mrs. Westerly. How may I help you?"

The boy's mother presented her hand. She beamed and bubbled. "I am Mrs. Addison Schyler; I am here to register for school. I mean, I am here to register Scott for school. I am his Mother." She tittered nervously. The boy saw Mr. Escobar roll his eyes to Mrs. Westerly; they had seen this kind of mother before.

Mrs. Addison Schyler's son, Scott, did not shake Mrs. Westerly's hand. Instead, he began to mindlessly stub a Frankenshoe against the bottom of the counter, a methodical rhythm that had surged through his soul for years.

"What grade?" asked Mrs. Westerly.

"His first year of high school." His mother's beam grew brighter.

Scott kicked. He was being childish, but when would he ever be given the chance to be anything else?

"Ninth grade," said Mrs. Westerly. She stifled a yawn. "Last name?"

"Schyler." Scott's mother spelled it out: "S-C-H-Y-L-E-R. Like SHY-ler. His father was Danish. It means scholar. Isn't that cool for someone starting high school?" When nervous, Addison Schyler could talk until the Tennessee cows came home.

Mrs. Westerly's yawn was now full-blown. "Excuse me," she said, "late night."

Scott responded with a double kick: Bam, Bam.

Mrs. Westerly peered at him in controlling—Stop that! —mode. "Take the stairs to the second-floor counseling office," she said, handing guest passes to mom and boy. "They'll set him up with—"

Another, louder thump resonated from the counter base. Mr. Escobar took a step toward Scott. Mrs. Westerly glared again.

"Stop that!" Addison's voice became a high squeal. She kept her smile, wishing to appear playful, but her eyes turned dark toward her son. She smacked the boy on the back of the head. The other two adults frowned, but they also shared another private grin. Scott kicked once more, less forcefully, and he withdrew.

Mrs. Westerly tried once more, "They'll set him up with a schedule." She settled back into her chair with a look of—Is it please Thanksgiving break yet? She barely glanced as the two walked away, Scott trudging behind his mother, but she added, "Welcome to Euclid High School, Mr. Skyler."

Scott's mother stopped abruptly; Scott nearly ran into her back. She pivoted angrily and announced, "It's SHY-ler!" She turned again, didn't wait for Scott, and stomped up the stairs.

Scott looked from mother to stairway to shoes. "Again?" he muttered. He began the climb.

THIRTY MINUTES LATER, after the bell ending first period had rung, and the second class had begun, Scott still sat in the counseling office. Mrs. Harris, his "personal advisor," she had said, "for the next four years" (*as if*), had questioned him about his interests (*none*), his past school experiences (*horrid*), and his plans for the future (*whatever Mother wants*). None of these answers were voiced by him; any answer offered was monosyllabic. Of course, his mother had told the story of Scott's brilliance and his Danish surname. He was finally given his new schedule.

During this time, Scott remained stone-like in Mrs. Harris' office. His back to the wall, he watched student passers-by through the office windows, on alert for any potential peril. The rambunctious sounds from the hallway, although muffled by the walls and windows, were a harbinger of almost certain confrontations. No matter how nice Mrs. Harris seemed, there was no way to wipe the new kid from the Frankenshoes, no way to stop what he had come to expect with every move.

When Dad had died—*Wow! Was it really six years already?*—he had taken with him any stability. Life had thudded to a stop. *Shouldn't I be over it by now?* Then: *How do you get over something that was your fault?*

Dad had died when he was eight. Mother found that she had to work for a living. She would start then stop. She would hear of a job, and they would pick up and move. Her flight response always had them on the wing. "I don't have anybody to lean on now but you, Honeybunch." Scott was not sure that was true, but he felt lots of pressure to fill his dad's shoes.

They had just moved back from Tennessee, a little place called Smyrna. They had lasted four months. He and his mother were stricken with culture shock. The food, weather, accents, schools, all were different. What was not different was work ethic. Having been told there were jobs at the car-battery plant there, Addison had gotten a job. Just a few weeks later, she had told Scott the chemicals were making her sick; she had quit. They had moved across town where she had found a job as a waitress, and where he had started new high school number two. Again, his mother had gotten "sick." She had lost her job and they had run out of money.

Out of desperation, they returned from whence they had fled: Englewood, Colorado, and a worn and shabby two-bedroom, one-bath apartment near his grandparents. It was not back to their own home, but at least it was close to people who cared. His grandparents had always tried to help, but his mother would not take advantage.

To her, it was all about appearances. Their attempts to help only seemed to tick her off. "We will do this ourselves," she had said. "You will go to school. You will be professional. You will excel." *And you, Mother?* It seemed easier for her to tell everybody else what to do than to do it herself.

To survive, Scott had created a plan. He would protect himself from the jerks, the assholes, and his mother, via the only choice that was left to him. To fight was to be punished by her; to talk back was to lead to fight. So, he would remain silent. He would walk down each hall in cautious awareness. He would be tripped, but he would not fall. He would be pushed, but he would not push back. He would duck his head like an ostrich in the sand and speak only when called upon. He would attempt to do everything as perfectly as he could to avoid any Motherly repercussions. Her standing orders were biblical: "Blessed are the peacemakers; turn the other cheek." To do anything but that was to call out the wrath of god herself.

Scott's mother and Mrs. Harris were finally done chatting. Mrs. Harris called to a boy sitting by the door of the outer counseling office, "Steve Martin?"

Scott adjusted his glasses and focused on a blond, compact, but muscular, kid. *Probably a wrestler.* The blond boy's fingers tapped frantically at his phone while his feet showed no sign of moving.

"Steve Martin, come here... Please." Mrs. Harris was attempting politeness, but Steve Martin was not so eager to respond in kind. Scott had heard the name before. *Some old comedian perhaps?* This boy did not seem like a comedian.

Steve Martin strode, reluctantly and with some arrogance, to Mrs. Harris's office. He said nothing while sizing up Scott, who tensed and stiffened into his seat.

Mrs. Harris said, "I'm assuming you have finished your work, Steve? If not, you shouldn't be on your phone. More important, I'd love you to graduate!" She smiled her best motherly—for me? —smile. Steve Martin did not reciprocate, rather, he frowned at having been called out in front of some new kid.

Mrs. Harris turned to Scott. "Scott, this is Steve Martin, he's my student aide this hour and he knows the school really well."

Scott knew all about student aides. Either A: they were smart, had completed required classes so they could graduate early, and now they had too much time to fill, or B: they were lost souls who would not spend their valuable time in class, and were put on a very short leash in order to be hounded, prodded, and begged into graduating, hopefully within the next six years. Steve Martin seemed to be the latter.

Mrs. Harris continued her formal introduction. "Steve, this is Scott Sky... no sorry, Schyler." *She pays attention!* "Would you show Scott the school? Then make sure he gets to Miss Walters' second hour English class: Room 306."

Steve Martin's answer oozed sarcasm, but with enough proper, "Yes, Ma'am," to make Scott wonder which was real. "I'd be happy to, Mrs. Harris." He limply offered his hand.

Uh huh. Scott stood and warily reached out to someone the likes of which he had known before. He would need to step here with caution. They shook cold and non-committal hands and headed for the door.

Mrs. Harris was not taken in either. "Steve?"

His smile waned as he turned back toward the counsellor. "Yes?"

"I expect to see you back here before the bell!"

The boy nodded. Scott stepped farther to the door, but his mother stopped him. She grandly held out her open arms. "Give me a hug, Honeybunch," she said.

Scott's left Frankenshoe fell like thunder to the worn linoleum floor. He shuffled back to his mother with a scowl. This was not what he needed Steve Martin to see or hear.

Mother and son met, shared a hug no more committed than the previous handshake, and the boys fled like two rabbits from a pack of wolves.

Less than ninety seconds later, the rabbits had reached Room 306. Steve Martin held out his hand with the schedule. He pointed in four directions: "North, south, east, west. You're a big boy, Honeybunch. You figure it out... Skyler." Emphasis squarely placed on the *Sky*.

Scott replied: "It's Shy—"

"Like I care!" Steve Martin sneered. "You got your schedule. You got your mommy! You're on your own now, Honeybunch!" He snickered, scanned the empty hall, and he pulled out his phone. Steve Martin looked Scott all the way up and all the way down, and then he snapped a picture before Scott could fathom how things had turned south so soon.

Blessed are the peacemakers pumped through his brain. His fists curled open and closed, open and closed. He turned red. But he remembered his plan and he did not move.

Steve Martin kept needling the new kid. "Whaddya bench, Honeybunch? Fourteen, fifteen pounds? You're scrawny. I could throw you..." He snapped another picture. "That's it! I'll tag ya: SlimScottScrawny." He spoke it as one name.

Scott towered over the smaller boy. *It would be so easy.* He took two menacing steps toward Steve Martin, who instantly backed away. *Thought so!* Scott was angry but would not be taken in—not today.

But he would remember. Steve Martin had made a crucial mistake. The *Slim* nickname was sacred. Only two people used it; one had been his dad— "So thin you can hide behind a noodle!" —always wishing he was as thin as his son. The other was his grandfather, Stanley, who carried on the name when Dad had gone, and who wished the same. Both men were sizable hunks. While Scott's lanky frame and accompanying ungainliness was imperfection that his mother abhorred, Dad and Grandpa viewed it as simple growing pains and remembered when they had been—slim.

But now, due to the wonder of technology, the whole school would know him to be Honeybunch SlimScottScrawny. *You're a real nice guy, Steve Martin.* All this, and he had not even made it to his first class yet.

Steve Martin backed away, guarded now, but still vengeful and still punching buttons on his phone. "Oh, and yeah, SlimScottScrawny?" He slithered over the words.

Scott tensed. *What now?*

The wrestler focused on Scott's feet. "Nice shoes, Honeybunch!" Then he was gone.

Scott stood alone in front of Room 306. How could those in the room not hear his heart beating? He contemplated his next foray into inferiority while his hand strangled the doorknob. He bowed his head to his chest and took a deep breath. He would go in; he would be professional, but not yet.

The hall was empty. Scott put his back against the grimy, red-brick wall and slumped to the floor. From his backpack, he took a worn, wooden Triceratops, rubbed its side like he had a zillion times before and thought of happier times. Even then, he rocked his head back and forth against the wall, beating time to what might have been.

2 | THE PROMISED LAND

A SMALL BALSA WOOD Triceratops, no bigger than a grapefruit—*Maybe one three-millionth the size of a real one?*—stared up at Scott as if asking "What next?" The toy, which was much more than that, was one thing Scott could depend on. Since his eighth birthday, the two of them had roamed, like the real beasts had about sixty-eight million years ago, across the prairies of Colorado and beyond, from apartment to apartment and from school to school, as his Mother had tried to find her way, dragging Scott with her. There had been little time to settle, to think, to mourn, or to repent... *Six years!* His heart, perhaps his mother's too, could not get past the loss of his father. Especially when he knew it had been his fault. At least now they were back where they belonged. Maybe they would stay. Maybe Mother would ask for help. Scott thudded his head against the brick. *Maybe. Maybe. Maybe...*

Both the Triceratops and Scott Schyler were natives to Colorado. Scott had learned that the Triceratops was first discovered in Denver in 1887. *Nerd!* Scott had started life more recently, just fourteen years ago, in Englewood, Colorado.

Scott's first eight years had been great. Dad and Grandpa, both named Stanley, had built Scott's first house. His dad was a carpenter, a trade he had learned from his father. The house was about a mile from Grandpa's in a pleasant older neighborhood. The house was red brick with white trim, with shutters around the windows. A sidewalk ran up to the front of the house, bordered by neglected flowerbeds. The lawn was brown against the hot Colorado sun. While neat enough, the whole yard needed some tender loving care. A detached two-car garage was in back, mostly used for Dad's tools. There was no room to park Addison's' Hyundai, which perturbed her.

Even as Addison wished to present a professional, well-kept appearance to the world, inside her home was a different scene. Dishes were dirty in the sink; clothes were in piles. "It is well lived in," Addison would say. But when it came time to ask people over, she would argue that "you cannot have guests over to a dirty house. I'm just too busy!"

Scott didn't see it that way. She was either on the phone all the time, or she said she was sick. Dad was always at work, but he would do what he could when he got home.

Scott wished to help, and Addison was more than willing to let him do that. Scott's chores were extensive, even early on. He washed dishes by standing on a chair in front of the kitchen sink. He would peel potatoes. "That's a very sharp knife. Don't cut yourself," his mother would say. *Mother, I was four!* He learned to fold towels; she even had him iron the handkerchiefs that Dad would take to work.

Mother had specific rules about chores: "If you use a toy, put it away. Do your chores first, then play." If he forgot or did something wrong, she let him know it with her voice, or her hand, or the belt. He tried extremely hard to never be wrong.

Scott's favorite thing about their house was his dad's office in the basement. Once you got past the laundry room and the furnace room, which was a scary place filled with odd sounds of machinery and things he didn't understand, he could enter the den. It was lined floor to ceiling with bookshelves and held the handmade, mahogany desk where his dad did all the bookwork for the business. Scott would play on the carpeted floor or watch him do math.

The biggest attraction in the room was dad's chair. It was an oversized, black-leather recliner. Scott played in it, and he loved to sit in it with his father. Before Scott went to bed, his dad would find a book or let Scott chose one. Scott would snuggle in his lap and listen. It was fun because Dad would play out the characters in each book. "...'And I'll huff, and I'll puff,' said the Big Bad Wolf." Dad would make sound effects, and Scott thought for sure that the pigs, or people, or dwarves, or dinosaurs were in the room. Sometimes, those huffs and puffs from Dad were real, but Scott was too young to understand.

Often, Scott could not play in the chair, or even downstairs, because his dad was sleeping. Dad would come home from work, saw-dusty and tired, and go straight to his basement chair. Sometimes he would not wake up until dinner; after, he would go back to his chair.

This bothered Scott's mother a lot. "You never pay attention. Don't you like us?"

Surely, if Mother said it, it must be true, and he wondered why Dad could not be bothered. Still, there had been good times. Times when his parents had laughed, and he had felt safe.

The best times were the weekends when the younger Schyler family would hold hands and walk together to his grandparent's home... unless Mother stayed home sick.

This house was the same shape and size, built from the same plan, but, somehow, it was warmer. Outside, Grandma Ray, short for Rayleen, liked to garden. There were flowers everywhere: irises, tulips, and chrysanthemums. Snapdragons were Scott's favorite because you could move their mouths; they had personality.

Inside, whether in the house or in the garage-turned-shop, Grandpa always had a project going. Now retired, he was a woodworker and carver. On the front porch was one of Grandpa Stanley's coolest creations. He had carved a golden eagle out of oak. It had intricate feathers, and the talons wrapped around its own tree branch. Standing almost five feet tall, with its wings spread across the porch, it had loomed over Scott when he was little.

Like Dad's stories, the bird seemed to come alive. Before Scott was big enough to understand, he had cried and shied away from the sculpture, hiding behind his father's legs. His mother pooh-poohed him, "It's just a stupid bird!

His Dad, however, would pick up his son and urge him to touch it. "What's his name? If you name him, Scott, he won't be so scary!"

Scott had thought about it, remembering a name from Sunday School. "Let's call him Moses." From then on, Scott had said "Hi" to the bird and patted it on the head before he went into the house. He did this now, then grabbed the screen door handle and entered. He let the door bang behind him. Here, there was no need to knock.

Grandma Rayleen's house oozed comfort. She and Grandpa Stanley had been married a long time. They had worked their carpentry business together, and often when Scott visited, they were still wearing paint-stained and Sheetrock-dusted work clothes, without any concern for how they looked to others. They had worked hard to create a cozy, but not extravagant, home.

At his house, it always seemed like Mother wanted more things, but she didn't know how to get them; she didn't appreciate what she had. Here, his grandparents had all they needed without trying. Scott struggled with the difference. Everybody seemed to work hard—well, Mother not so much. But was that the big deal? Scott wondered if it was just that his grandparents smiled at each other. *How could that be? How does that happen?*

"Grandma?" Scott shouted unnecessarily, as he sought her out. Grandma Ray was where he knew she would be, in the kitchen. She emphasized that this was not because she was a "little wife and homemaker," but because she liked to cook.

"Hey, Little Bear!" she said, as he approached.

Scott didn't think of his grandma in age or appearance. She was older—sixty-something probably—but fit from the work she still did and never dirty; she was as neat herself as was her house, but again, it didn't seem as if she had to try so hard.

What Scott knew about Grandma was how he felt, secure and loved; she *was* home. She was always his first stop. "Hi, Grandma," he waved.

She smiled, waved back, and motioned for him to take a seat at one of the bar stools at the kitchen counter. She may have said she was no "little homemaker," but she did exactly that. Bubbly and always in good spirits, she took care of them all.

Scott aimed for a stool, but only after pausing for a generous hug. Grandma herself was cozy and comfortable. He was almost as tall as she was, and he would stand on tiptoe to meet her eye-to-eye. The warmth he received was awesome, and he relished any chance to experience it.

The next thing on the agenda? Cookies! There were always options, like Grandpa's favorite: burnt sugar. These were not a favorite of Scott's due to the molasses, but they were edible. Better? Scott's favorite was chocolate chip. Even better? Add a glass of chocolate milk! This was a Schyler do-it-yourself tradition, not to be forsaken. "Grab the Hershey's," his grandmother would say. "Three teaspoons only and don't spill; stir it in good." He liked to watch the dark, oozy stream mix into the milk before he stirred it. Sometimes, he was not so accurate and got more chocolate.

"You'll just spoil him," his mother would say.

Grandma would answer, without acrimony, "That's what I'm here for!"

Scott wondered what the difference was between spoiling and love.

TODAY, MOTHER AND FATHER walked, Scott skipped, down Cherokee street. It was his eighth birthday, and Scott anticipated a new bicycle. His dad's old Schwinn was creaky and rusty; it was time to get an upgrade.

Scott was fascinated with the street names in his neighborhood. His grandpa had told him that they were all named alphabetically after Indian, rather, Native American names: Acoma, Bannock, Cherokee, Delaware, Elati... Grandpa had told him that if he memorized them all, he would get his bike, plus maybe a couple of other surprises! Grandpa was helping, and he had made it to Mariposa, Navajo, Osage, and Tejon. *Only six more to go!*

Jumping the three steps to where Moses sat on the porch, he left his parents in the dust. Mother called after him, "Don't slam the door!" He slammed the door. He didn't see her disappointment, nor did he see his dad's disappointment with his mother.

Stanley Jr. left his wife and slowly walked around the side of the house towards the garage. Scott's dad was six foot four, he wore a grizzly bear beard that Scott played with, and he very often whistled. Today's tune was *She'll Be Comin' Round the Mountain*.

Addison mounted the front steps alone and entered.

Inside, Scott raced toward Grandma. They shared a stupendous hug. "Are you ready to be eight?" she asked.

Scott nodded. She handed him three cookies. "He's in the back," she added.

"They're still warm," Scott said. He smiled as he grabbed three saucer-sized... "Hey, these are chocolate chip!"

"You..." she smiled, "...get one. Don't slam the door!"

Scott moved through the back door, careful not to slam it—much. He took the three steps in one leap and scampered to the detached garage in the back.

The overhead door was wide open, and Grandpa Stanley met his grandson there. He was panting hard as he brushed dirt off his clothing. "Hello, young man!"

"Hi, Grandpa!"

Having worked all their lives as carpenters and builders, both Stanleys had been rugged outdoorsmen and in good shape—for a while. Grandpa Stanley towered over Scott, even taller than his dad, at six–seven. He was also very round. Over the years he had settled down. His athleticism had moved to bulk, much around his middle. "I make a better door than a window," he would often joke, self-conscious at his own size. Age, Grandma's cooking (or too much of it), less strenuous work, and concerns with his heart had turned what had been a sizable two-hundred eighty pounds of construction worker muscle into three-hundred seventy-eight pounds of giant teddy bear. He lumbered when he walked and breathed heavily all the time. It was a constant battle to will himself to move.

Grandma Ray tried to, good-naturedly, chide him into doing something. She, doctors, and her son had been increasingly worried that someday his heart would give out, but Grandpa Stanley was a man set in his ways. Working out and dieting were "against my religion," he would say. It was because of all this that he had continued to call Scott, as did his son—Slim. "You can both remind me; maybe to think thin is to be thin!" he would say.

Stanley Senior tousled his grandson's head. They waited together as Stanley Junior's whistle drew closer. Stanley Junior waved to Stanley Senior and then, with an awkward expression, he stopped mid-whistle, pulled up, stood up tall with arms akimbo, and took in a sizeable breath.

Scott and Grandpa Stanley walked toward Stanley Junior to see what was wrong.

The three met on the sidewalk. "You okay?" asked Stanley Senior.

"Yeah, I just ran out of breath."

"From whistling?"

"I'm not sure... I'll be alright." He looked at his father's grimy clothing. "What have *you* been doing?"

Stanley Senior replied, "I had to move a wheelbarrow of dirt for your mom. She's going to kill me yet..." He inhaled, "...what with all her flowerbeds!"

"It's not her flowers that'll put you six feet under," said his son. "Please be careful. I don't want to have to dig a hole for you!"

Stanley Senior said, "Me either. You'd be diggin' for days!" Both men grinned as they walked back to the garage."

Scott looked from one to the other as the two men bantered. Scott hugged his grandfather and handed both men a cookie.

"Thanks, Mr. Slim," Grandpa said before taking a bite. He broke off half of his cookie and handed it back to Scott. "I don't need the whole thing; it'll ruin my dinner. 'Sides, one of these things'll kill you they're so sweet!"

His laughter was infectious, and they all caught it, but his son added, "You sure got a lot of dying on your mind." He was attempting humor, but his dad's health was always a concern.

"It's the dirt," replied Stanley Senior. "Give me wood chips and sawdust any day." He took a bite of cookie; crumbs met sawdust on his overalls. He continued, "Nope, if I die it'll be from your mom's cooking. Blame her!" He chuckled again.

When Scott's grandpa said stuff like that, it never sounded like he meant it. *How could that be so different from my mother?*

The three stood and munched. Behind the large man, and in neat order around the garage-turned-shop—which would never see a car—were a drill press, band saw, table saw, and a myriad of other tools all placed for maximum efficiency. At center was a worn, walnut workbench, well-lit and covered with wood shavings. Scott could get lost in this room, and he was hoping that someday he would learn what all the stuff was. He saw a new project sitting on the bench. "What's that?" Scott mumbled through a mouthful of cookie.

They moved to the bench, and Scott peered at a large, twenty-four inch by eighteen-inch block of blond wood that was taking a curious shape. From what had started as a rectangle, four new feet—tiny paws—were emerging. They appeared to be grasping something. The paws, and what looked like a wee bit of nose, were reaching for the overhead light.

Scott said, "It's upside down!"

Stanley Junior asked, "Is that maple?"

Grandpa Stanley was finishing a bite. He began to explain but got cut off by his wife's voice from inside, "Come and get it!"

He stopped chewing, swallowed, breathed deeply, and said, "We just got our dessert. Now we get dinner?"

Scott scrambled before them up the back stairs. "It's party time."

"Oh, yes," huffed his Grandfather, reminded of the day. "Wait for me, Slim!"

Scott was already inside.

No more than half an hour later, after fried chicken and German Chocolate Cake, another of Scott's favorites, Scott had opened presents. He had finished by reciting the street list, ending with Umatilla, Vallejo, Wyandot, and Zuni. The family realized there was no X or Y. "Why is that Grandpa?" Scott had asked, but no one seemed to know. The group had applauded, then they had behaved like the party was over. Scott's smile turned to disappointment. *Where's my bike?*

"It's outside," said his dad with a grin.

They all moved to the front porch where a large package was stashed behind Moses. *Had that always been there?*

Scott grinned but looked questioningly at his Mother.

"Go for it," she said, "save the paper."

Stanley Junior countermanded the order, "Just dig in, Scott!" Addison was not pleased, but she kept quiet.

Scott dug. He uncovered a baby-blue, twenty-six inch, Roadmaster Mountain Bike aired up and ready to go. *Who hoo!* He bumped it, tire by tire, down the front stairs.

"This block only," said his mother," we'll talk about rules later." *Of course we will.*

Stanley Junior looked at her as if to say something, thought better of it, and nodded in agreement.

Scott had learned already on Dad's old bicycle.

Now, he had one of his own. He took off like a shot. Out into the street, down the street, up the street, and back again. He roared into the driveway a few minutes later feeling set for life. Cookies, cake, and bicycle, what more could any eight-year-old ask for? As his grandma watched from the porch, he hopped off the bike and flung it onto the grass.

Grandma Ray called to him. "Pick it up, Scott." He did.

"Walk it to the side of the house." She pointed to the gravel next to the driveway. "Stand your bike there." He did.

"You'll be safe; I'll be safe; your bike will be safe. Are we clear?" Grandma had her rules too. That was okay by him. She explained them. What she said next, however, was not clear. She pointed to the shop and said, "Be sure to keep all your fingers."

Puzzled, Scott ran around the house and met his dad and grandpa inside at the bench. He hugged his grandpa's middle and said, "Thank you!"

"You're welcome, Slim. Good job on the street names... Were you careful? You gotta be careful about Bannock!"

Scott nodded vigorously "I was. I didn't get close." Bannock was no man's land, forbidden passage. It was much too traffic-congested for a little boy.

"Slim," his dad said, "we're not quite done yet. You think you can handle more?"

Scott's eyes widened. "Sure!"

Stanley Junior said, "So take a look."

The conversation began where it had ended before the party. Scott looked at the wood block on the bench and asked again, "So, what is it?"

"An otter," Grandpa answered." And to Stanley Junior, "Yes, it's maple."

"How do you know?"

"What?"

"That it's an otter?"

"Listen."

"What for?"

"Shh! Listen." Grandpa Stanley placed his finger to his lips and looked intently at the eventual otter.

The workshop went silent except for the breathing of the three. Grandpa made the silence go on a long time. Scott fidgeted.

Finally, Grandpa spoke. "Do you hear it? It's chattering through the maple. There's an animal in there that wants to be free."

Scott was not sure what to think, but when Grandpa spoke, he was learning it was good to pay attention.

Dad asked, "How old are you?

"Eight."

"Wanna whittle?"

"Mother says it's a stupid hobby."

"Your mom can have her own ideas. I asked you."

"Will it be okay?"

Grandpa sighed deeply. Dad asked, "Are you here with me?"

"Yes."

"Do I know how to whittle?"

"Yeah, but you don't do it very much. Grandpa does a lot more than you." He looked around the room. "I mean, look at all the cool stuff."

Stanley the Younger smiled and looked at Stanley the Elder. "Retirement is a good thing!" Both men laughed.

Grandpa took over. "Try not to use *stuff*. What's a better word?"

"Uh..." Scott thought. "Things?"

"Better. Another?"

Scott scrunched his face. "Uh... Items?" Grandpa could be particular too!

"Good. When you go to do something, be clear on what you want. It makes it easier."

Dad asked, "If you could carve something, what would it be?"

Scott was eight; there was only one thing to carve. "A dinosaur!" he answered with glee.

"Okay. Now, be specific. What kind of dinosaur?" asked Grandpa easily. "You just start carving; you'll make a mess. What do you want to see in the end?"

Scott knew exactly: "A Triceratops!"

"Good. What's the first thing to do?"

"Get wood and I need a knife," Scott blurted.

"That's two things." Grandpa was all about precision. He slowed Scott's dash toward the Cretaceous Period. "No. First you're going to close your eyes."

Scott squinted them shut with only a hint of—"huh?" It *was* Grandpa.

"Now, you're going to visualize the Triceratops.

What do you see?"

"I see a—"

"No, don't talk, see, visualize. Think about your animal. Look at each leg; see the body; notice all the markings of the head, the tail, all the things that make a Triceratops a Triceratops. Do you see it?"

"Yeah, but there are parts I don't remember." Scott started to open his eyes.

"Keep 'em closed. Keep looking. You're not doing it all at once; everything happens in its own time. Now, open your eyes."

In front of Scott sat a new block of balsa wood. It was the perfect size for eight-year-old hands. Right next to it...

"A pocketknife!" Scott cried. Scott reached for it eagerly, but his dad placed his hand firmly on Scott's arm.

"Slim, it is not a pocketknife," Stanley Junior said sternly. "It is a whittling knife. It is a tool. "Actually..." he held the knife so Scott could see the handle, "...it was my first whittling knife. I thought now was a good time to give it to you."

Scott looked at the wood-burned signature on the handle: Stanley Scott Schyler Junior. Scott was impatient to hold it, but his father continued, "It is very sharp and very dangerous, and you will use it properly or not at all." He stopped and brought his eyes to firmly meet Scott's. "Do I make myself clear?"

"Yes, Dad." Scott could not hide his disappointment.

Grandpa asked, "Are you ready to start?"

"Yes."

"Alright, here's how you start." Stanley Junior handed Scott the whittling knife, birch-handle first, and showed him how to hold it. Its blade was about two inches long. It did not fold like a pocketknife but was kept in a leather scabbard. Next, he reached into his shirt pocket. He said, "The knife is not the most important tool. Here," he said and handed Scott his second tool.

"A pencil?"

"Everything happens in steps. Like Grandpa says, if you start cutting without a plan, you'll just make a mess. So, the first thing you have to do is sharpen the pencil." He showed the boy how on the first pencil, then offered him a second so Scott could do it himself.

All eyes were on Scott. He held the pencil in his left hand and the knife, blade away from him, in his right. He took his first cut and watched a shaving fall; he took a second and a third. *Hey, I'm doing okay!* Now, he dug too deep and snapped off the nearly sharpened tip. He pouted at his dad. He was almost in tears. "I'm sorry, Dad.

"Scott," said his dad, "have you ever sharpened a pencil like this before?"

"Well, no..."

"Then don't be so tough on yourself. It's okay to mess up. Just take your time."

Scott tried again and managed a good point.

As he was finishing, Grandpa Stanley took over again. "Your dad's right, Scott. It's okay to screw up, but it's better to plan ahead. To do that, you're going to use the greatest tool you have. Here's the block of wood; you've got your pencil... "Now, close your eyes again."

Scott did as he was asked.

"Now, look at the Triceratops from the front, from the side, from the top, and from its rear end. Those shapes are wishing to be set free from the wood. Pick a side to start on."

Scott nodded.

"Open your eyes. Which side?" Grandpa asked.

"The left," answered Scott.

"So, you're going to draw the left side on the left side of the block, all the little details down to the hoof marks on the toes. You got that?"

"But what if I mess up?"

"That's why the pencil and the eraser. And there's one more thing."

"What?"

"Before you start, you want to be calm, in control, well prepared in your noggin. He tapped the side of his head with a large, meaty finger. "To do that, you need to breath: slowly, steadily." Grandpa showed him. "In through the nose... Out through the mouth... Count to five each direction."

Scott thought this was kind of silly, but he did what he was told. As he saw his elders do the same, he thought it might not be so silly.

They breathed together, although Grandpa's was strained and wheezy.

"Now, see the left side of your animal; draw the left side, slowly, steadily."

Scott followed directions.

His dad broke in. "You guys go on. I'm going to go lay down."

"But Dad?" said Scott. His father placed his hand on his son's shoulder.

Grandpa Stanley asked, "Are you sure you're all right?"

"Just tired," answered the younger Stanley. He trudged off to go inside.

Grandpa Stanley reached for his otter-to-be and his own carving tools. Slim Scott sat next to him under the lights. For a long time, until it was almost dark, and Grandma called them in for dinner, the two worked together, one creating a clam-opening, fun-loving water mammal, the other fashioning an eight-year-old's version of a balsa wood dinosaur. Occasionally, Scott would ask a question. His grandfather would answer. But for most of the time, the two sat and worked a hobby in wonderful and powerful silence. Scott wished that dad had stayed to whittle as well.

3 | Brocco-Roni & Cheese

Addison Schyler was aghast. "My son will not use a carving knife! He is eight; he will cut his fingers off. You must be out of your mind!" She pulled her hands out of soapy dishwater and shook them furiously at her husband. Scott was supposed to have washed dishes before they had gone down the street. "Birthday or not, he should do his chores!"

Scott's father had been gearing up for this battle. "He's my son too!" He took a deep breath to try to calm himself. "You have him peel potatoes all the time, and chop vegetables too. I taught him how to hold the knife; I'll teach him—"

Addison cut him off like she was slicing a tomato. "A bicycle is one thing, but a knife? He is a kid. He is clumsy. He is never paying attention."

Lately, Mother and Father had been having too many of these noisy conversations. They didn't seem to agree on anything, especially when it was about him. *Am I that much trouble?*

Scott edged away from the conversation and toward the living room. He looked at his fingers. He still had all ten. Now he understood what his grandmother meant. He held the sheathed knife in one hand, gripping it hard for fear of it being taken away. In the other hand was the balsa block, the nose of a Triceratops just forming. He was really taking his time and wanted to do it right. He had wanted to work on it all night, but his parents had said no.

Addison banged a pot into the dish drainer. "As for Saturday, it is already arranged. Bethany at the agency worked hard to get Scott his timeslot. She says he is smart and well-mannered and has 'the look' they want. He will get free food and meet some other kids, and Bethany says he could become a famous spokesperson. She knows people! You do not wish to be a part? Stay home. My son and I are going."

"A spokesperson? Are you sure that is something Scott might want? I was hoping he'd go to work with me on Saturday, I could use a little help."

"But Scott is really looking forward to this..." she said.

"I am?" Scott whispered from the other room.

"...He can go do your work for you some other time." She plunged her hands back into the suds, and the conversation was over.

Scott's dad exhaled in defeat and walked into the living room. He stopped and placed a hand on his son's shoulder, where it remained for a long time. He saw the blade in Scott's hand. "You be careful," he said and walked toward the stairs.

"Do you want to read, Dad?"

"Not now, Scott." His voice faded as he descended.

Scott dissolved into his room. He placed the Triceratops and the knife on his table and wondered what to do next. He had promised he would not work on it without someone being nearby.

He opened a little kid's pop-up book his parents had given him when he had started to read. They had even signed and dated it. With every page you turned, a new dinosaur sprung up. It was still his favorite book. He began to study the dinosaur pictures, wondering what he should carve next. *Next? Finish the one you have!*

He found himself humming, *She'll Be Comin' Round the Mountain*, as his father had done earlier. His left hand rapped pleasantly in time, on the wooden desk his dad had built for him. The more intently he studied, the more intent became the rapping.

His mother came into his room without knocking. "Hey, Scott."

He set the dinosaur book, open and face down, over the knife. He did not look up at her. The humming stopped; the rapping did not; its tenor turned from pleasant to irritated.

"Can you stop for a minute?" Addison asked. "You did not do the dishes like I asked. I wanted to tell you 'happy birthday' all by yourself, but I do not want to treat you to a fun day if you do not do your work. Are you ready for Saturday? I'm excited!" Her non-stop chatter drilled into his head.

Scott nodded with little enthusiasm. He wondered why he was always in trouble. Every time they talked it got itchier and itchier. It felt like when he had gotten into poison ivy. *Just make it stop!* He was his mother's rash. Sometimes, it seemed like he didn't matter at all and going to this audition was not going to fix things.

"Do we have to?"

"Honeybunch, Bethany says it could be a big break. She likes how tall and slender you are and how your eyes sparkle. She calls it camera presence. You have the chance to be seen by thousands of people."

Scott drummed his fingers on his desk and avoided eye-contact. Bethany was weird. She and Mother had been in high school together and hung out sometimes, but mostly, they talked about stuff on the phone, like spa dates and JLo and Justin Timber-somebody. Now, Bethany wore stringy neon-blue hair and finger-nails that clattered because they were so long. Scott thought she looked like someone out of a science fiction movie. She worked for the *L'Orange Advertising Agency*. Scott remembered this because his mother pronounced it importantly with a sweep of her hand, "Low-raw-nge." She said the word sounded "snobbish," whatever that was, but she was jealous that Bethany made so much money.

Scott had no idea what he was getting into, so he said, "Dad doesn't think I need to go—"

"Your father does not get it. I want my son to be somebody important. There will be bright lights and cameras. People will see what a special boy you are."

Sure, if your kid's a star, you'll get noticed too! Mother had told him many times that she had wanted to be an opera singer. He had heard her sing and thought, with eight-year-old ears, that she was good. She would tell everyone how she had trained professionally as a musician, how she had been headed for the stage, how life turns on you by the choices you make, like marriage and a kid. He had heard her say that a lot! It seemed to Scott that she was never sure what she really wanted. He thought of Grandma's house again, simple and pleasant, but for his mother, never enough.

"So, what do I have to do?"

Addison perked up at her son's interest. "You know how I have taught you to speak clearly to others and present yourself well?"

"Yeah..." Scott was wary.

"That's all you have to do. *L'Orange* sells things to people. Bethany says they have a new product for kids, and they need kids to present it. All you do is read and smile and eat. You are good at all three."

That was true enough anyway. But showing off with other kids? It sounded noisy, with lots of people he didn't know. *Was it necessary?* He would rather spend time with Dad or Grandpa. "Can't someone else be spokesperson?"

Addison would not be swayed. "Bright and early Saturday. It is you and me. Make sure you get all your chores done." She left him without a "goodnight."

A week later, Scott's mother rousted him out of bed. "Scott, the audition is live; we have to be there on time. Up and at 'em. Let's go. Let's go!"

Scott reluctantly put on his best dress clothes. He fidgeted with the tie his Mother had pulled from Dad's closet. He gave up tying it and conveniently "lost" it under the bed.

"Let's go, Scott! Now!" She yelled from the other room. You would have thought it was her audition.

They left the house at the same time Dad did: 7:30. Dad hugged him and told him to have a good time. His mother and his father didn't kiss or even look at each other.

L'Orange had rented a studio at KLLZ TV, in downtown Denver. Mother drove. They traveled mostly in silence. Addison drove the car into a big parking garage and grumbled. "My son is going to be a star, and I have to pay? Who do these people think they are?" She paid and parked. Her door slammed and she took off. Scott ran to catch up.

Inside the offices, Addison announced their arrival. "Hello, my son, Scott, is here... Scott Schyler."

"And you're here for?" The disinterest in the lady's voice behind the counter was palpable.

"Why, for *L'Orange* of course." His mother seemed shocked that the woman didn't know.

"Follow the sign." The lady gave his mother a strange look, pointed and moved on to those behind her. "Next?"

Welcome to L'Orange! Mother and son followed a large yellow arrow to Sound Stage number four.

At the entrance to the sound stage, Bethany, wearing a big, floppy, purple hat and with heels to match, met them. She looked perfect to play greeter at a kid's birthday party. She and Addison hugged. "I'm really, really glad you're here," Bethany fawned. "I've put in a good word to Mr. Farnsworth. This should be a lock." *Then I could have stayed in the car!*

Bethany led the two across the studio floor, past

three cameras on rolling tripods. People stood behind them with headsets on. Scott wondered what that was all about. The room was brightly lit, but the walls were bare except for a banner at the back that read: Brocco-Roni and Cheese! Give us more please! Under the banner were three rows of countertops with space to walk between them, each higher than the one in front. Behind each counter was a folding chair.

Bethany, after having to convince Scott's mother that parents were not allowed beyond the cameras, led him to the center of the top tier, probably, he thought, because he was so tall. "There you go, Scott. Have fun." She left him to seat someone else.

Scott stepped up and struggled to squeeze around the other chairs to get to his own, without knocking any over or falling off the tier. He sat down, glad to be far away from center stage. Already he was taller than anyone he knew at school, and he hated being in anyone's way. Here, he would have the chance to keep his head down and try to not get noticed. This was tough to do when his mother kept waving from offstage.

Around him, seats began to fill with seventeen other kids of various shapes and sizes—six to a row. Most of the kids were yelling, but a small, fuzzy-haired blond girl next to him on the right was the screamiest. She was maybe six or seven, and she wore yellow—brighter than a lemon under the sun: yellow frilly dress, yellow bows in her hair, yellow matching shoes. Her attitude matched her apparel.

Someone must have told everyone that to be loud was to get the part. Scott thought he had missed that memo. "Rah," he said, mostly to himself and watched the show.

Scott tapped his fingers on the Formica while listening to unrecognized music that blasted around the room. He scanned the parents and kids, trying to match them up. The blond was easy, her mom was also a lemon. *Eew!*

Scott gathered information about who he was up against. He was only eight, but he had always been sensitive to what was happening around him. Most of the kids were well dressed, probably their parents were richer, their lines more rehearsed, their demeanors more camera-ready. They would have the better chance. *For what? Am I competing? Do I even wish to be spoken to?*

The stage lights went brighter still. Scott squinted from the glare and pushed up his new glasses. He hated these. The lenses were thick and edged with black plastic. He could see better, and he did not seem to run into stuff, er, things as much, but he still felt other looking at him like he was a geek.

Through his glasses, what he saw—what he felt—felt fake. He might not have been able to voice it well, but the feeling he got working in silence with his Grandpa was totally different than all this. It seemed like everybody here just wanted to be noticed, and no one genuinely cared. Scott discovered proof of this on the counter right in front of him; it was a simple piece of masking tape with his name scrawled on it in Sharpie. No one really wanted to know him. Though he was only eight, his young soul understood he was only a small part of a big game.

A woman stood to one side of the center camera and spoke into her headset. She began to count down: "Three...two..." Scott was intrigued as she pointed, then only mouthed the word, "One." This was so her voice would not be picked up by the microphones. At the same time, a light on top of the center camera came on. Above the stage and directed to the audience, the APPLAUSE light also flashed on. Parents and kids cheered, and out scurried two people. The first he knew. It was Bethany. She ran into the room like a cheerleader at a Bronco game, her purple hat flopping around her ears. The second was a man he had not seen. He was smaller than his dad (but who wasn't) at about five-seven. His hair was silver-gray, on both the top and his pointy beard too. He looked like the guy on the KFC chicken bucket. He was well dressed in a three-piece, white suit, but he wore an overlarge bow tie the same color as Bethany's hat. *Aah, how sweet, a matched set!* What Scott was drawn to most, however, were their faces. Their phony, made-up smiles reminded him of clowns at the circus. He was beginning to feel like one of the caged animals.

"Hey boys and girls, I'm Fred Farnsworth..." said the man, waving to the eye of the camera. The studio audience cheered and whooped as did the eighteen youngsters seated, but jumpy, behind the duo.

"...And I'm Bethany! We're really glad you're here!" There was more whooping. The light on top of the second of three cameras blinked, the signal to perform for whoever might be watching.

Bethany began to pass out three by five cards to each child, smiling all the while. Fred explained the process. "I am Fred Farnsworth," he said again. "I am owner of the *L'Orange Advertising Agency*. Can you all say *L'Orange*?"

Eighteen children ages five to fourteen, and some mothers too, shouted in unison, "*L'Orange!*"

"I want you to know," said Farnsworth, "that you are on TV. Everything you do is being recorded so we can find our next star. I want you to be polite, listen, and when we come to talk to you, we want you to speak clearly and honestly. Can you do that?"

Again, the youngsters cheered. The energy level was intensifying and so was the racket. Scott felt the cage bars closing in around him, but he played along, wondering how this would all work. He realized he was hungry. They had not had breakfast, but his mother had said they would get fed. At least that was something to look forward to.

A camera blinked on; this time it was Bethany who spoke. "Alright guys, raise your hands if you like macaroni and cheese."

Seventeen hands shot up. One more raised timidly. *Mac and cheese for breakfast?*

Bethany grabbed a microphone from the center cameraperson and went to a young boy in the front row to Scott's left. The boy was about Scott's age. He had brown, curly hair, and he wore a Justin Beiber *Sorry* T-shirt. *Must be his mom's.* Then: *So much for dressing up.*

She held out the mic which the boy tried to take. Still smiling, she pulled her hand back and said, "Hi..." She paused to look at his name, written on the masking tape on his countertop." ...Luis! Are you happy to be here?"

"Yes." His voice was barely a whisper.

"Luis, I really need you speak up for us please and talk into the mic, okay? Let's try again." Bethany walked away and stepped back to the boy. "Hi!" she said again, as if they'd never met, "What's your name?"

Luis sat up straight and yelled, "I'm Luis." Scott could hear a Spanish accent now.

"Are you hungry, Luis?" Bethany asked.

"Yes, miss."

"I can tell by your accent... Do you speak Spanish, Luis?"

"Yes."

"That's really awesome! We need someone to present Brocco-Roni and Cheese to our Hispanic demographic. Do you see the card in front of you, Luis?"

Luis looked lost, but he nodded and picked up the card.

"Luis, I'm going to ask you to do three things now..." She turned to someone off-stage. "Can we get the product now please?" She waited impatiently while eighteen microwavable bowls and eighteen sporks were placed on the countertops. She sighed when, finally, her helpers had everything set and she could continue.

"Luis, when I say go, you're going to do three things. First, you're going to open the package, gently and completely. Take the whole wrapper off the top and place it by the bowl. Next, you will take the spoon and dig into the bowl for a big bite. When you do, you want to look really excited and really hungry. This is the best stuff you have ever eaten, okay?"

"Yes," said Luis.

"Then third, you are going to eat your bite. Chew really quick but show us how much you love it. Then you will read the card. Can you do that?"

"I'll try," said Luis.

"Great, here we go. Are you ready? Everybody else needs to be really quiet, okay? Go!"

Scott raised his head as Luis began. The cover was tricky, but Luis finally got it open and dug deep with the spoon. So far so good. Luis lifted the bite to his mouth and chewed. He got a strange expression on his face, but he smiled through it. Now there was just one more step: to read the card. With a mouth full of green pasta, Luis read, "No more plain old mac and cheese. Try Brocco-Roni and Cheese, eat veggies with ease. Broccoli and carrots and aged cheddar cheese, veggies in pasta? Give us more please!"

Luis had made it through. He had done exactly what he had been asked to do. The problem was that he still had so much of the stuff in his mouth, his slogan came out more like, "Nomopla macandchees... Brocholandcartsssandchedchese..." He did nail the last line, "Give us more please." But by that time all was lost. Snickers started and grew until they were full-blown laughter. Scott tried not to laugh, but it sounded funny. But he also felt bad for the other boy; even the parents were laughing at him. It was how Scott had felt many times, and he hoped someone would stick up for Luis.

Farnsworth glared at Bethany, motioned to the floor director who shouted, "Cut!" then turned his wrath upon the young actors. "Knock it off all of you!" The child actors drew quiet while Farnsworth talked in adult. "We are on a deadline. Time is money and you will not waste my time. The Brocco-Roni campaign is huge for my company..."

Farnsworth had not mentioned Luis. Scott thought that was rude. He bowed his head and drummed his right-hand fingernails on the Formica countertop. He glanced at his masking tape nametag, and he made a decision. With his left hand, he began to scratch off the tape. He crumpled it into a ball and dropped it onto the floor. This would make it impossible for Farnsworth (and maybe Bethany too), to identify him. *They're not going to call on me anyway.*

He picked up his spork and began to use it as a drumstick on top of the Brocco-Roni container. The sound was a dull plastic thud, thud, thud that drowned out the drone of the advertising executive.

A purple hat appeared in front of him, and Scott started. His drumming stopped even as Bethany said,

"You need to stop and listen." She gave him a death-stare. "This is a really important chance for you. Your mom has promised. Don't let us down." Her head and hat whirled with finality as she retraced her steps toward her boss.

"Mr. Farnsworth, are you ready?" Bethany called across the stage. He nodded, and the director yelled, "Quiet on the set!" and began the count. *Welcome to Hollywood!*

Bethany pivoted her purple to the tiers. "Who likes Brocco-Roni?"

Seventeen children raised their hands and shouted, "I do!" The eighteenth began to smack the container with his spork again. He shook his head.

Bethany, oblivious to Scott's behavior, zoned in on the yellow-garbed, fuzzy-headed dynamo to his right. "What's your name, little girl?"

The girl oozed like syrup over an IHOP chocolate-chip pancake. "I'm Amanda," said Amanda. She should have careened into the ceiling from her energy explosion.

Bethany winked at the camera and motioned for Amanda to settle down, "Why, of course... You're Amanda." She rolled through the sentence like a snide French waiter. She pimped for the camera, sharing a little inside joke about how she really felt about the overly exuberant Amanda, even as she talked to a little girl who could not understand the implication.

Scott barely heard the conversation, one where Amanda was asked about her pet: "a labradoodle," and her favorite color...

"Wait for it... I think we can guess..." said Bethany.

"Yellow!" Amanda squealed with glee.

Bethany rolled her eyes for the camera, then she asked Amanda to mimic what Luis had done. "Now Amanda, you'll open the package, take a bite, make sure you chew well so you can speak well..." Here, she turned to Luis whose head was still bent in his shame. "...Remember, it tastes great! Then you will read your card. Okay?"

Someone had prepared Amanda well. She gushed, "I'm ready!" as she sat on the edge of her seat.

Bethany backed out of the shot and said, "Go!"

Amanda glowed straight into the camera, pulled the wrapper, took a bite, chewed in as elegant a fashion as one can chew and read, "Cauliflower and peas, in our macaroni and cheese? It's new Brocco-Roni and Cheese, Give me more please!" She froze her smile, as if she had done this a thousand times, until she heard the word "Cut."

The studio exploded in applause. Yellow Mom was on her feet. Even Scott was impressed. But he also knew this was not for him. His mother had told him this would be fun. People would see him and think he was special. She had said he was there to be somebody. That they all were. He began to rock back and forth, rapping his knuckles on the desktop to the cadence in his head. Scott thought about the Whos, Dr. Suess's Whos, from Whoville. They were constantly shouting, "I'm here, I'm here!" The difference was, the Whos *had* to be noticed to survive. For Amanda, for Farnsworth, for Bethany and for his mother, it was all a big show.

Scott's antics drew the attention of the co-hosts. Amanda shied away from him and quit smiling, at least for a second. Farnsworth called out with disgust, "Let's take ten."

In an instant, whatever friendship and camaraderie there had been with the guests burst like helium balloons floating too close to the stage lights. Farnsworth started to make moves on Yellow Mom while Bethany reached for a cigarette and headed in Scott's direction.

He immediately realized his true value to the world around him. He was just a prop. He was not there because he was special. He was not there to be celebrated for some grand accomplishment. He was only there to be used to sell Brocco-whatever. And he had not even had the chance to eat any.

Scott put his head down, ostrich-like, as Bethany advanced. *I'm not here. I'm not here.*

It didn't work.

"So," asked Bethany through a cloud of smoke. "Are you always this rude?" She didn't wait for an answer. "You are really making this tough on your mom! How old are you?"

Scott coughed through swirling smoke and pushed up his glasses. "Eight."

"And are you a good kid? Your mom says you are smart. I'm really not seein' it. Do you do what Addison tells you?"

Do I have any choice? "Yes," was the spoken version.

A purple-hatted puff of smoke pressed closer to

Scott's face. "Do you want to stay here?"

How can I even get close to that truth?

Bethany continued, "In about a minute, the cameras are going to switch back on, and Mr. Farnsworth and you are gonna talk. I want you to smile; I want you to follow the plan. You have the looks, but do you have the attitude? This is a really big deal for you." Bethany's grin grew smarmy. "Will you help me? Your mother will be proud of you."

"Uh-huh."

"Good!" said Bethany, transforming back into Ms. Fun With Purple. "Mr. Farnsworth, let's start with this one." She dropped her cigarette butt to the floor in front of Scott, crushing it under an outrageously pointy shoe.

"Will do," Farnsworth answered and crossed the stage. "Hello, young man," he said, not impolitely. Then he looked at the countertop. "Where's your name tag? Did you remove it? How am I supposed to know who you are? What's your name?"

Scott pressed the silent button. This guy did not know him, nor did he want to.

Farnsworth lost his patience and said, "Well, if you're gonna play that way, I'll just call you..." He looked Scott over from head to toe. "...Slim!"

"We'll go in ten, Mr. Farnsworth," said Bethany.

Scott went white. Knuckles rapped the counter. His best friend, his dad, called him Slim. This guy was not his friend. Scott's anger breathed through him in short shallow gasps.

The director motioned; Farnsworth nodded and waited for the count, then he addressed the children. "Are you big fans of Brocco-Roni?"

Cheers and pleas erupted again. Then, Farnsworth turned on Scott. "Are *you* a big fan of Brocco-Roni?

"I... I don't—"

So, Slim, what grade are you in?"

"It's not Slim." Scott murmured.

"Why, I bet you're in third grade? Most of the good little boys and girls here are in second or third grade. Right?" He spun to watch as the other kids went crazy again.

The noise and Farnsworth's condescending attitude had Scott's head pounding. He spoke quietly. "It's not Slim, it's Scott. Only Dad and Grandpa call me Slim."

Farnsworth ignored him. That was worse than anything. It was Scott's turn to shout, "I'm here." But, for his mother, he held his tongue. Instead, his larger-than-the-average-bear fists now beat the countertop: Once, twice, three, four times.

Fuzzy yellow girl jumped away in fright. Farnsworth stopped mid-stride and looked back at an enraged boy. Bethany, who had moved to stand next to Addison, cringed in embarrassment.

"Cut!" Farnsworth called. He leaned into Scott. "Listen, I don't care what your name is. Show me what you can do, then we'll be pals. Okay?"

Scott felt that that would never happen, but he nodded reluctantly.

"You know how this works, Slim. Wrapper, spoon,

chew, read." He took a step back. "Cameras ready?" He paused to make sure and sneered. "You're on."

Scott planted a big false smile, just like Amanda's, on his face. He stared into the camera while he ripped off the label. Whatever was in there was now cold. He grabbed his spork, small even in his third-grade hand, and took a bite. Scott's jaw clenched. *Wow, that's... That's...* He could not find the words, but he kept the smile and forced the stuff down his throat. The card was in front of him, and he picked it up to read, chewing and thinking and trying not to gag. He began, "Smooth and creamy and green..." And then he changed it. "This stuff is shit, if you know what I mean."

Bethany looked at Farnsworth in shock. Addison's jaw dropped. She turned red and looked ready to explode. Scott was done with Brocco-Roni. He stood, knocking over his folding chair which clattered off the tier and onto the concrete behind him.

Amanda screamed. Yellow Mom dashed to her aid.

"Cut. Cut. Cut. Cut. Cut." Farnsworth hung his head. "I hate kids," he said.

Scott jumped off the back of the stage and headed for the exit sign. Too many critical eyes, including those of two ad execs and his mother followed him in astonishment. The boy did not stop until he reached the parking garage. He sat on the hood and cried as he waited for his mother. Brocco-Roni was not the way he wanted to be noticed.

4 | Arrythmia

IF IT HAD NOT been for Brocco-Roni, Scott thought, all would be well. But he knew that was not true. He looked up and down the musty, dim hallway of Euclid High. No one had bothered him while he sat on the floor outside Room 306. A couple of students had passed by. They barely saw him; they probably thought he was someone in trouble who had been sent to time-out. Teachers did that.

He knew he should go inside, but he was having trouble getting past, well, his past. Instead, he took a deep breath, and then another. *Slowly, steadily. In through the nose and out through the mouth. Count to five each direction.* His Grandpa had a knack for this. Sometimes it worked for Scott, sometimes not. Today, not so much.

THE RIDE BACK FROM the television station had not been pleasant. No "Honeybunch" from Mother this time. The Hyundai Sonata was too small, too enclosed, for the anger that was churning between him and his mother. The throbbing pressure of loud against his ear drums forced his head away from the noise. His breath fogged the passenger window.

Addison spoke, saying the same thing she had said sixteen times already, "This was supposed to be fun. You had the chance to be cool and to make friends and to show all the stuff you know. I was embarrassed! And that girl? She was scared to death. I can't believe you couldn't control yourself enough to..." She paused only to turn the corner, her mouth racing as fast as the car. "...Be a gentleman. Is this what I taught you? How could you do that?" Her voice trailed and wavered with disappointment. "All you had to do was sit there, answer a couple of questions, smile and..." She passed a semi. "...Are you listening to me? What were you thinking? Didn't you want Grandma and Grandpa to be proud?"

"He was a jerk!" sneered a tearful Scott.

"Who do you think you are? Here was a chance for you. I was excited for you. What do you do? You yell at Mr. Farnsworth! Really? You yell at Mr. Farnsworth. You may have cost Bethany her job!"

What? No more L'Orange...?

"On TV! You about killed that cute girl next to you."

Right, Mother.

"And then you walk off!" She braked for the light. She stared straight ahead; her hands clenched the steering wheel.

Scott turned toward her, took a deep breath and wished to speak, not to yell. "You didn't hear what that guy was saying to me—"

"It doesn't matter. You are polite and professional. They are the adults, with jobs to do and you're just a dumb kid."

"I'm not dumb!" Scott attempted to stick up for himself, but it came out whiny. "*You* say I'm smart. I just wanted—"

"It doesn't matter. You were dumb today. I have never been so embarrassed. You were so rude."

She turned onto Acoma and pulled up in front of the house. She hit the brakes as she ran the front tire up on the sidewalk. Scott was tossed forward. He caught himself and pushed his jostled glasses back into place. The driver's side door opened, then crashed closed. Mother was gone.

Scott yelled through the closed car windows at the top of his lungs, "I'm here! I'm here!" He banged his head on the dashboard in rhythmic thuds with enough energy to trigger a hundred airbags. Tears came to his eyes. He wished to be seen for who he was, not this way. *How do you get someone to listen?*

He sat a couple of minutes, ages in eight-year-old terms, and tried to calm down. Eventually, he opened the Hyundai door and made his way into the garage. Dad was not home yet, so he could not talk to him. There was only one place to go. He grabbed his bike and took off. *Mother won't even know. She won't even care.*

The peddles churned as he worked south down Acoma Street, the street he lived on, past the Tastee-Freeze and the Methodist church. He turned right, toward Cherokee Street and the love of his grandparents. They were not that far away, but they were miles from his unhappy reality.

He pumped with purpose. Every turn of the chain around the gears released some of his anger. He knew he would be in trouble when he got home; he was not supposed to ride across Bannock, a dangerously busy one-way street, but today he didn't care. You had to cross Bannock to get to Cherokee and that was where his grandparents were. He pumped harder.

He stopped at Bannock, his long legs straddling the bike. Cars flew by. Scott's heart beat faster. Part of him said, *Just go; get it over with.* But the other part told him there must be more. *Yeah? How do you find it?*

He looked both ways. He started once and had to stop as another car came speeding over the hill. He looked again and stepped hard on the pedal to gain momentum. *Whew! Made it!*

He didn't look back. He turned onto Cherokee and continued to the house where he dumped his bike in the yard and scrambled up the stairs.

He stopped, looked around as if to remember something, and retraced his steps. His attitude steadily improving, he picked up his bike, neatly propping it against the side of the house. He rebounded up the steps and paused to pat the giant eagle. "Hello, Moses," Scott said soberly.

He grabbed the screen door handle and went through, letting the door bang behind him. "Hello, Grandma."

Grandma Ray sat at the kitchen counter. She did

not smile. Instead, she motioned to him to be quiet. She was on the phone, and whoever she was talking to did not seem to be offering good news.

She asked the voice on the other end, "What is it again? Well, can you spell it please?" She grabbed a note pad and began to write. As she did that, she turned aside to Scott and whispered, "Go get your grandpa, please." She motioned toward the shop, then continued spelling out a word: "A-r-r-h..."

Scott missed the rest of the spelling as he ran outside. A minute later, he and Grandpa climbed the steps. Grandpa was a few steps behind and grasped the rail to pull himself up, huffing and puffing. Grandma Ray met them.

"Hey, Little Bear, I need a hug." She looked at her husband. "You too," she said. She stopped in mid-hug and looked around. "Where's your mom?" she asked. Her already concerned look deepened. "Did you come alone? ...Across Bannock!" She looked at Scott in shock. Whatever she had learned on the phone was bad; he had just added to it!

She sat down heavily. "You know you're not supposed to cross—"

"I had to, Grandma." The safety of this place allowed Scott to spill his guts. "I messed up, Grandma. This guy called me Slim and no one else should. He was not nice. I made Mother mad at me because I embarrassed her, and she called me dumb, when I'm not, and I'm not supposed to be here, so I'll be in trouble again. Can't I just stay here, Grandma? Please?"

She looked at him, but she was thinking about other things. "Stay here?" said Grandma. "Stay here? Scott, you could have been killed." She blinked at him as tears formed.

Grandpa Stanley put his arms around his wife's shoulders. "What's up?"

"We've got to go." She blinked again and rubbed her eyes to clear the tears. "Your son is in the hospital. I'm not sure Addison knows... Scott, you should not have..." She stopped on the edge of heartbreak, but she didn't let go. "I can't lose both of you on the same day!"

Stanley Senior gasped. "What are you saying?" He forced himself to breathe.

"Stanley checked himself into Metro this morning. You know how weak and tired he's been feeling? I just got off the phone. The doctors say he has an arrhythmia. He was driving home and had to stop his truck; his chest hurt so bad."

"So, he's still alive?" asked Stanley Senior. He was still wrapping his head around what she had said, "... lose both of you."

"What?" She stopped and realized his confusion. "Oh, yes, he's okay, but they had to shock his heart." Then, it was as if the doctors had just shocked her heart too. Grandma Ray's attitude snapped from distress to action. "Scott, put your bike in the garage and lock it up. Stanley, call Addison; I need to see my boy." She was on a mission.

Scott looked on in a daze. He was frightened, and it was all happening too fast.

"Scott, do what I asked. Go, now!"

Now I've made Mother and Grandma mad! He stepped out the door, grabbed his bike and did as he had been told. He met Grandma at Grandpa's truck parked in the alley. They waited for Stanley to get there to unlock the doors.

"I'm sorry, Grandma—"

"We'll talk about Bannock later," Grandma Ray said, none too pleasantly. The doors clicked as Grandpa walked around the corner of the building. "Get in!" she said to Scott.

The two waited as Stanley pried himself into the cab. He rarely drove anymore; his large belly made it uncomfortable to be behind the wheel. He tugged at the seat belt and put the key in the ignition. Scott saw all this and thought about arry... "Grandma, what's arrh-yth-mia?" He struggled to get around the word.

"Your heart gets out of rhythm, sort of like a ticking clock. Your dad's heart apparently didn't want to tick today." She attempted humor as she didn't want to scare her grandson. "The doctors are working on him; he'll be okay." She sounded hopeful, but Scott was not sure she was convinced.

Grandpa shifted the truck into reverse and backed into the alley. He straightened the truck and spun gravel. "We'll pick up Addison on the way," he said.

"How come?" asked Scott.

"How come what?" Grandma replied, "Use why instead of *how come.*"

"Why is Dad's heart not beating right?"

She took a deep breath and struggled to explain it in eight-year-old terms, even though she was really speaking to Stanley Senior. "It might be hereditary. Um, Scott, that means it gets passed on from father to son. It's called cardiomyopathy."

Scott tried the word to lock it in his brain, "Card-io-my-o-pathy. "Why's it so big?"

Grandfather Stanley answered: "It's Latin. Doctors use lots of Latin. It keeps things very specific and clear. Every word is exact."

"But how come two words?" asked Scott. "Sorry, why?"

Stanley Senior slowed the truck to turn back to where Scott had just come from, so Grandma Ray answered, "Arrhythmia can be caused by cardiomyopathy."

Scott worked to understand it the best way his smarter bear could. "So, Grandpa, you gave Dad a bad heart that won't beat right? Are you both going to die?"

Grandfather looked at Grandmother. The tension coursed across the front seat. Grandma Ray's mood turned cold. "That's why I try to get your grandfather to move more and lose weight and eat better."

Grandpa Stanley stopped the car, none to gently, in front of Scott's house. He growled, "Scott, go get your mother."

Scott leapt from his seat and closed the pickup door. Now he was trapped. He didn't want to hear the rest of his grandparent's conversation. He hardly ever saw them fight and it made him squeamish. He would much rather have the hugs. But he also did not want to face his mother. There would be no hugs there at all.

He slowly climbed the three steps. Addison had told Grandpa she would meet them, but apparently, she was not ready yet. He slowed down. Since his grandparents were there, maybe Mother would not be so mad. *Fat chance!*

Scott opened the door and yelled, "Mother, c'mon. Grandpa's waiting!"

Addison came out of her bedroom, and she immediately opened up on her son. Her fear mixed with anger and there was only one place for it all to land. "Keep your voice down!" Her tone was menacing. "Three weeks. No bicycle, no knife, no grandparents. Are you kidding me?"

"I'm sorry, Mom—"

"You're sorry all right. Tell that to your father. I do not need to go to the hospital for two of you. We can't even afford one."

She barreled past him to the door and right on through. "Come on! We are late!"

Scott stood for the briefest of moments, wondering how his dad getting sick had been his fault.

The ride to the hospital had not gone well. Addison was still angry about *L'Orange*, and about Bannock. She also seemed to be put out about having to go see her husband. "What did he do now?" she had asked.

Scott's grandparents were still angry about how Grandpa was too fat, so they didn't say much at all to Addison, telling her not much more than they had told Scott. They didn't seem to know much yet anyway. The four rode most of the way in silence; their hearts beating for the well-being of a father, a son, and a husband.

THE HALLS OF DENVER Metropolitan Hospital were crowded. People walked by all wearing the same kind of outfits and wearing badges. The building smelled like Grandma's house after one of her full-on Saturday cleanings. It was not a bad smell, but combined with all the people scurrying around, it was not near as comfortable.

The elevator ride to the fourth floor was, at least, a nice change from the tension. It was all glass and faced Downtown Denver and the mountains. The sunshine was blazing through the glass and warming the whole car.

When the doors opened, Scott's mother was first out. She sped to the nurse's desk. "I am Addison Schyler. I am here to see my husband, Stanley." Her tone was curt and rude. Scott didn't see the need for it.

A nurse, dressed in blue like almost everyone else, checked a big whiteboard on the wall. "He's in room 4412."

Addison glanced around at the room numbers and turned sharply in the proper direction, but the nurse stopped her.

"Oh. But wait." She stood and walked around to the front of the counter. "If you could all follow me please."

She walked down the hall in the opposite direction, then she stopped at the door of a glass enclosed conference room. The nurse opened the door and said, "If you would all have a seat, I'll let the doctor know you're here. He'd like to speak to you first."

Grandpa Stanley asked, "Everything is okay isn't it?"

The nurse hesitated. "Better the doctor explains, I think." She closed the door before anyone could ask any more.

Scott was anxious. "Grandma?"

His mother gave him a nasty look.

His grandmother sat down, her back to the windows and to the world. She said, "Well, that doesn't sound good."

"Let's be calm and just wait and see," answered her husband. He sat down heavily next to her and pulled her to him.

Scott moved to stand near his grandfather. All were silent.

Addison lowered herself in a chair opposite and looked past them to the city. She became uncomfortable in the silence and asked, "What do we know about his truck? Is it alright?"

Really? Scott's jaw dropped as he looked at her.

"Really?" Grandma Ray spoke the thought. "That's all you can think about?"

"Oh, stop!" Addison answered. "We cannot know anything until the doctor gets here. I just thought... It's a brand-new truck!"

The three stared at her.

A timid rap at the conference room door caused Scott to look up. He pushed up his glasses to see better. His mother swiveled her chair to see the doctor, who was a slight dark-haired man who also wore glasses. They were round and perched on top of his head. He had a yellow stethoscope around his neck. Scott had heard that word, and he wondered if it was Latin too.

The doctor spoke quietly, "Mrs. Schyler?"

Two voices combined. "Yes."

Mrs. Addison Schyler glared at Mrs. Raylene Schyler and took charge. "I am Mrs. Schyler; I am his wife!"

The doctor looked at each of them. "I'm Dr. Velson." His gaze stopped at Scott. "I'm wondering if this might be a lot for a youngster," he said. "Maybe one of you'd like to take him outside for a couple of minutes?"

"He'll stay here. He's old enough," said Addison. "Maybe he can learn something. Sit down, Scott." He found a chair next to his grandfather.

"But Addison—"

Addison ignored her. "What's the deal, Doctor? When can I see Stanley?"

Dr. Velson took a moment, rolled a chair over by Addison's side and slowly sat down. "There were complications. He had a heart attack in his car and pulled over. He should have called nine-one-one. He drove himself here. How he did that I'm not sure."

"He's a tough strong man, that's how," said his mother.

"Perhaps" said the doctor, "but sometimes we

all need help." He paused. "He fell in the parking lot. Another patient found him, and we wheeled him in. We shocked him then, and in the emergency room." He stopped again and pointedly looked at Stanley Senior, "Has he had any symptoms before this?" He studied each face, thought better of waiting for an answer, and he continued. "In any case, his heart muscle has slowly been deteriorating."

Grandpa Stanley's voice was a thin rasp as he spoke, "Are you saying...?" He stopped. Behind him, the sun went behind a cloud. He gasped for air, as his wife held him for dear life.

Dr. Velson nodded. "I am sorry for your loss."

Scott thought the air-conditioner had just turned on. It was colder than January on this August day. No one spoke. Scott looked from face to face. He looked at the doctor who looked back at him. "I'm sorry," Dr. Velson said to everyone. He stood and left the room.

Scott's mother had backed herself and her chair away from the doctor. Her face was white. Scott could not tell if she was angry or sad. She just stared out the window.

"Mom?" He looked to her, but she was unavailable. He turned to view his grandparents who were deep in their own grief. They had latched onto each other the way Grandpa clamped two boards together in the shop. Both quietly sobbed.

Each person was in their own private place; there was no place for him.

Again he wanted to scream "I'm here!" but he knew

he didn't have the right. He was alone, and he realized it was his fault. It was his mother's fault.

Scott's feet churned a mournful rhythm of IF underneath the polished oak table. IF they had not gone to the stupid audition, he would have been with Dad. IF he had been with Dad, he could have called nine-one-one. IF he had not ridden his bike past Bannock, his mother would be talking to him now and telling him what to do. IF he had not gone to Grandma's house, they would not be crying and angry.

He looked for compassion from around the room, but he knew why he could find none. Scott's heart hurt. He thought of blood flowing through his father's heart, *or not flowing, I guess.*

I did this. I did this. I did this.

It would take some time, but eventually he would realize this was not true.

5 | To Be Mediocre

SCOTT SCHYLER'S FATHER had died a week after Scott's eighth birthday. That had been six years ago. It had hurt then; it hurt now. *Is there any way to get past this?*

Scott remained on the floor, in a dirty hallway, outside a classroom in Englewood, Colorado.

He studied his Triceratops as the beast looked up at him with one lopsided horn. He had hurried, like Grandpa had told him not to. He had cut too quick, too deep. *Sort of like my mother makes decisions!* He had thrown it across the room because he was not perfect. He had angrily stabbed the workbench with his carving knife. The blade was still bent, but at least it was still usable.

The knife had been perfect, and then was not. His dinosaur had been perfect, and then was not. His dad had been perfect... Every step of the way had been due to Scott's imperfection. *Why should I even be around?*

GRANDPA HAD SHEATHED the knife and put it in his pocket. "You are smarter than that, Scott," he said. He had picked up the dinosaur, still a work in progress, and held it in his large hands. He examined where the horn had been broken and looked at his grandson. "Hey, Slim, this can be repaired. But not today…"

Scott had argued, "But, Grandpa, I'm sorry, I'll use it better. I promise."

His grandfather had pulled up a workbench stool and they had sat together. Stanley's breath slowly wheezed in and out as he had sought the right thing to say. "Two weeks, Slim. You'll have to prove that promise. I have always tried to never promise unless I can do what I say I will. You think about how you can repair this."

Scott pouted. "I can't!"

Stanley Senior sighed. "Everything can be fixed, Scott. Sometimes it takes time…" Then, he said, "But Scott, you have got to control your anger."

Obviously! Or we wouldn't be having this conversation! Then: *Oh. Now, I'm angry at my grandpa?* Grandpa was seldom angry. Scott wondered if his grandfather even knew how he felt at all.

Grandpa Stanley answered the boy's unasked question. "Listen, Slim. I know you're angry at your father and your mom and at yourself. I'm mad too. Why did my son have to die? Why wasn't I there to help him? Was it really me that caused his heart condition?"

"You think that too, Grandpa?" Scott asked.

"Scott, you can't think your dad's death was your fault! Sometimes things just happen. I hate to say it this way 'cause it sounds so stupid, but it's just true. Sometimes there is no reason. We all have flaws, your dad's heart, my heart too, I guess…" He rubbed the belly of the little dinosaur. "Your Triceratops horn too. No, we all have flaws. But we have to learn from our mistakes." He had handed Scott his carving. "When you get your knife back, you can fix and finish this guy. He's coming along nice. Then you can try something new."

Now, Scott itched his back on the brick wall outside Room 306. He squeezed the scratched and scuffed round body of his balsa friend tightly. He was glad he had listened, but it was tough knowing that no matter how perfect you tried to be, mistakes still happened. He felt like sneering at his grandfather's words— "That's why they make erasers." *Ugh!*

Scott had continued to carve and sand and stain and learn. Even as he and his mother moved, he had kept in contact with Grandpa as best he could. He had worked on a Stegosaurus, then a pterodactyl, which was a lot harder, because of the wings. Scott thought it was just okay, but his grandpa loved it. Grandpa Stanley had hung it over the work bench where, like Moses on the front porch, it kept watch as the two worked.

Lately, his attention had been diverted. He had not thought about carving in a while. Maybe he would find a good subject to carve and try again. Especially since he was home.

He took a Grandpa breath, in through the nose and

out through the mouth; count to five each direction. He stood up and put away the animal. It was time to try again.

He clenched the doorknob to Room 306. Inside the room, he heard voices as students were doing what they do. He prepared to enter and remembered his mantra for survival: He would remain silent. He would speak only when called upon, and he would try to do everything right.

He turned the knob. Nothing happened. It was locked. School security. *Always on guard from people like me.* Now he would have to knock. It was the polite thing to do, the professional thing to do, his mother would say, but it would also draw the sixty or so eyes in that room directly to him and his Frankenclothing. "Damn!" he muttered.

Before he could put knuckles to door, he heard a commotion inside the room.

"Someone's at the door; I got it, Miss Walters." Whoever this was, he was not one to ask for permission. Barely a second later, the door swung open. A roundish, bubbly boy said, "Sup?" He was about half Scott's size, both up and around, but his presence was bigger than life. "Are you here for English class? Are you ninth grade? Man, you're tall!"

Scott didn't answer. He stepped into the room, feeling enormous and more bumblier than ever. He held out his schedule to the teacher.

Miss Walters said, "Rodney, your exuberance is entrancing,"—she loved her big words— "but please, for the fourth time, sit down!" Rodney's bright countenance went to minor shadow. As he sat, Miss Walters continued, "I'm sure this gentleman can speak for himself."

She raised her chin to look up at the boy. Scott looked back with fourteen-year-old awe. Miss Walters was gorgeous. She was well dressed in a tan skirt and orange sweater—right for the season. Her attire seemed natural, unlike his pretentious mother who wore high heels to go to the store. Her body was shapely, her black hair framed her face perfectly. And she smiled at him!

He had seen too many teachers that showed up like they had just gotten out of bed. Miss Walters was not one of them. Her face glowed, even though she had just yelled at Rodney. Scott already liked how down to business she seemed, in control of the room and the situation.

"Hello there. What's your name?" she asked.

"Scott. Scott Schyler." *Only when spoken to!* He showed her his schedule.

"Well, Mr. Skyler, oh wait, did you say Shy-ler? Welcome, Mr. Schyler, to Introduction to Literature and Composition." She looked around. He followed her gaze, and together they discovered the only empty seat was front row center. "If you'd take a seat, we'll continue," she said."

Scott wanted to tell her that was a bad idea, but he held his tongue, took his schedule back from her and squeezed into the blue-plastic, combination desk/ chair. *Who was it that thought high school students could fit into these things?* Trying to get settled, he stretched his long legs into Miss Walters' walking path.

"I can't see!" Announced a young lady directly into his ear, one of the many students he had not yet noticed through his fog of apprehension.

Scott scritched his neck, adjusting his glasses to try to see who was behind him, but it was just a glance. Miss Walters made a speedy decision. "Okay, Sarah, no need to shout. Stand up."

Sarah obediently stood.

"Scott," stand up."

But I just sat down! All eyes were on him. With a perturbed sigh he untangled his legs, climbed out of the desk, and grabbed his backpack. Some students chuckled to each other. Scott had no doubt the comments, toward him and about him, were derogatory. He hung his head to avoid eye contact and tried to be smaller.

"Now," said Miss Walters, "trade places!"

"But Miss Walters—"

"You'll be okay, Sarah. Change is a good thing." Miss Walters smiled and then, not so accommodatingly, added, "Now move. Please!"

Sarah and Scott maneuvered around each other while the rest of the class watched and got squirrelly.

As they both resettled, Scott had a better chance to view the girl. She was pretty, but not too—rah-rah, cheerleader pretty—which was okay with him. He did not like their— "I'm here!" —attitudes. Sarah had red hair, but not fire engine red. *What was the word? Auburn?* An elegant word, according to his mother. He could tell the girl was studious because she had to move three textbooks, two library books, and an instrument case, along with her make-up, and, of course, her phone, to the basket underneath her chair. *Girls with all their stuff!* No, *not stuff, property.* He was in English class, after all.

As they sat, Sarah's eyes had met his, then they had both looked away. It was only a millisecond, but there was something about the way she had looked at him. *Interest or loathing?* Either way, it was obvious she was out of his league. *How would I even begin a conversation?*

Scott's knees touched the underside of his new desk; his feet had nowhere to go but to the filled rack below Sarah's seat. He kicked it once, by accident. She turned and glared at him. He kicked it again in answer. She started to tell him to knock it off, but her eyes met a cold, silent gaze. She turned back without a word and moved her books to make room for his feet.

Miss Walters brought the class back to the subject at hand. "Who can tell Mr. Skyler here what we've been working on?"

"It's Schyler," said Scott quietly.

Miss Walters let that pass as she searched for a hand. Of course, Rodney's hand shot way up. He did not wait to answer. "We're making meaning by understanding vocabulary," he said. He had read the daily learning goal right off the board.

"Thank you, Rodney, for reading to us, but what does that mean?"

"You have to use the right words to make what you say make sense," said a squeaky someone in the back.

"Yes, April," answered Miss Walters, "and to figure that out, we are working on understanding this article from a man named Koestenbaum." She stopped and looked at Scott, who squirmed in his seat. "Mr. Skyler, I'm going to put you on the spot and ask you to read what's on the board for us." She pointed to the quotation. "Will you do that please?"

Already? Scott stalled and looked around. He also remembered his own rule: speak when called upon. It was the only way. But his disappointment in an English teacher who didn't remember, or care about, his name was growing, and he let Miss Walters know it.

"It's SHY-ler," he emphasized and then read what was on the board. "Some people are more talented than others. Some are more educationally privileged than others, but we all have the capacity to be great."

Scott's voice was smooth and clear as he continued. *Professional. Do it right!* "Greatness comes by recognizing your potential is limited by how you choose, how you use your freedom, how resoluted you are. Greatness comes by your attitude. We are all free to choose our attitude."

Scott stopped, breathed a deep sigh of relief, and looked at Miss Walters. She and her class were taken aback. Who knew that voice and that ability was inside this shy, gangling boy?

"I apologize, Mr. Schyler. I'll try to get your name right, I promise. That was very well done. Had you read that before?"

"No." *Speak no more than necessary.*

"Well, you read very well, especially extemporaneously. So, Scott, what do you think of what you just read?"

He lowered his head and put his right hand slowly to his desk. He began to tap in thought, his long middle finger doing a quiet thump, thump, thump. If he said too much, he was a schoolkid. If he said nothing, he was a pain in the butt to the teacher. His mother would be less than happy with bad grades. He feared his mother the most.

Miss Walters waited. "Scott, you don't have to be right. It's about what you think."

He read the piece again and decided he was not sure he believed Mr. Koesten-whatever. "I'd have to change a word, Miss Walters," he answered.

This put his new teacher on guard. Many ninth graders would not even attempt to understand the saying, much less comment, for fear of being wrong in front of their classmates. While Miss Walters wanted her students to think things through and to dive deeper into something more than just a video game, it was often difficult to get them interested. Yet, here was a young man ready to offer analysis. She took the chance, "And what word would that be?"

"Mediocre."

Titters of discomfort sounded from those who did not get it. Young high schoolers were not known for their deep thinking. Miss Walters was shocked at the honesty. "Mediocre?" she parroted, "How do you mean?"

"We all have the capacity to be mediocre. We all think we're great, but it's just a lie."

"Tell me more."

"My mother says it's all for nothing. We try so hard to do the right thing. She says, 'Vanity, vanity all is vanity.' Everybody says everybody's a hero, but only one in a million are really great. Attitude's not going to change anything!"

"That's awfully harsh, Mr..." She made sure to get it right. "...Mr. Schyler. Do you think you're mediocre?"

He didn't want to say what he said next, but Miss Walters had drawn him to it. "On a good day. Usually, I'm not even that."

The class again snickered uneasily. Many felt inside what he had voiced, but they would not admit it.

"Hush!" Miss Walters wanted thoughtfulness. She also wanted to steer Scott to a truth. "Look, you just started us off on a really good discussion. Isn't that great?"

Sarah had turned almost out of her chair to be able to see him better. Their eyes met, then they both quickly retreated.

"Nothin' better than anyone else might have said." He turned quiet and tapped on the top of his desk again. He could hear the chatter behind him; he had said too much.

Miss Walters walked to his desk and focused on this intelligent young man. She pressed still harder. "Certainly, you think you are good at something?"

He could *not* say, "Sure, good at killing my dad." He felt the pressure from his peers, and he would not offer anything more.

Scott saw Sarah begin to pack her books; apparently, the bell was preparing to ring. Some students even started to stand up. Miss Walters did not stop them, and she kept her eyes on Scott, intrigued by this thoughtful newcomer.

Scott felt it was rude if he didn't answer, so, barely heard, due to the bell and the clatter of desks and feet and the cacophony of student voices, he muttered, mostly to himself, "Drums. I'm good at the drums."

Whether she had heard him or not, Miss Walters touched him on the arm as he stood and said, "Thank you for your thoughtful sharing." She smiled and walked away.

Scott was confused. He had been expecting more from the teacher, some sermon perhaps on how you should be, *who* you should be, but that had not happened. He was not sure how to react. He pulled out his schedule and headed for the door.

Students spilled out into the hallway chattering and yelling, the pandemonium punctuated with hoots and hollers and plenty of stares at the scrawny, head-over-everyone new kid. Scott tried to ignore them as he sought out, and spun the combination to, his new locker. He took from his backpack a worn pair of drumsticks and stuck them in his back pocket.

As he did he noticed, only seven clanging locker doors away, the girl, Sarah, talking excitedly to a friend. He overheard snippets: "too tall;" "so quiet;" kinda..." The voices faded.

What? Kinda what? Sarah's scattered giggles and her eyes on him made him nervous, and he peered into his empty locker.

"Hey, Skyler, er, Spiller, er..." The voice of Rodney bounded toward him. Rodney saw the drumsticks and shouted, "Cool, I'm in band too!"

Big whoop. Scott attempted to ignore him. He placed his backpack inside the locker and closed it. He adjusted his glasses and looked up and down the hall, not quite sure which direction to take.

Rodney, tenacious as a car salesman, continued into his big mistake. "Hey, Skyler... What's your name? Ah, screw it. Hey, Slim!"

Scott Schyler's eyes found Rodney's. Scott Schyler's foot found the locker. He did not just slam it, he kicked it like the peddle of a bass drum, not once, but three distinct beats. Suddenly, Rodney found himself backed against the lockers, gripped around the neck by some exceptionally large hands. The hallway din muted around them and Rodney's face paled.

Scott's tone was as smooth as had been his reading of Koestenbaum, the pace as slow as molasses over cornbread. "I do not like to be called Slim."

Scott felt this was nicer than how he had treated others in the past. He did question why the nickname was so important to him, but that didn't take much thought. *It's all I have left.* Scott dropped Rodney about ten inches. He stalked off with a zillion eyes in attendance.

Rodney, perhaps more persistent than smart, simply shook it off and called after the tall one. "Well, whoever you wish to be... Here, Miss Walters wanted you to have a textbook!"

Scott stopped, wheeled around, and scowled. *What a pest!*

"Remind me to do you another good deed sometime!" said Rodney. He rubbed his neck while handing Scott a battered literature book. "Let's go to band!"

Stepping back to his locker, Scott reopened it, placed the book inside, and closed the locker again while Rodney waited. *This kid must be lonely to hang around with me.*

Scott followed Rodney into the flow of traffic, not sure what to think. *Pest maybe... What does he have that makes him so... bubbly?*

Me? Always on guard. Always aiming for mediocrity. Is it just me?

The words, "Greatness comes by your attitude," pealed like a bell.

It can't be that easy...

His hands closed tightly around his drumsticks which were, along with the Triceratops, the most important things he owned.

6 | Sproingy-Thingy

"**I**'M GOOD AT THE DRUMS," he had said. That might have been the first time he had dared voice his belief aloud. Long before *L'Orange*, before the Triceratops, and before his dad's death, there had been the beats. Shy tippy tip of snare, raucous clang of angry cymbal, or throb of heartbeat-like tom-tom, there was always rhythm flowing through Scott's soul.

He had been too young to remember how it began, but his Grandma Ray had told him the story of the sounds that were becoming a part of who Scott Schyler wished to be. The precision that he was finding in woodworking, and even in his studies, had always been a part of him. How it began to present itself was as early as when he was in diapers, and it would be found right at his very own doorstop.

It had started early on a Saturday. Scott's mother and father were lounging in bed, smiling and cuddling, appreciating a little alone time. They were discussing their baby boy and the wonders of their life together, albeit shaded with the burden of new responsibilities. Someone asked, "Are you going to get him?"

"I'll get him."

"No, I will. You did last time."

Obviously, neither one wanted to move. They had not heard anything yet from the nursery, so they relished the quiet while they could get it.

Scott had, according to Grandma, just turned two. He was learning to walk and was into everything: exploring, prodding, and poking. And now, he was up. From his room, came a curious sound—Sproing.

His parents looked at each other. Stanley said, "I'll go see."

Addison said, "I'll go see.

The odd sound happened again—Sproing and continued—Sproing, Sproing, Sproing...

Stanley threw back the covers with a quizzical look, as did Addison. They looked at each other and said in unison, "Let's both go see!"

As his parents neared Scott's door, they about fell over one another trying to avoid stepping on their boy. Scott had escaped his crib and had crawled to the bedroom door where he had found something brand-new and wonderful.

Scott had discovered music in the bit of spiral metal that kept the nursery door from banging into the wall. He would tap the doorstop with his already long fingers, hear its Sproing, and giggle. He had made something happen, even though it would be impossible for him, at that point, to describe what it was. He stroked and stroked the rubber-coated spring, watching it flap back and forth, and listening for each Sproing. Something in the pace and the rhythm charmed him, animated him. He looked at his parents as if he had found Wonka's Chocolate Factory all by himself.

His parents had watched him for a while; they even

took video of his antics. Then, his mother had picked him up. Something had changed within her. "Don't you know that's dirty?" she asked, holding him away from her like a soiled puppy.

Scott started to cry in her arms, and he reached back toward the floor.

"But he's having fun," Stanley Junior countered. "Hey, Slim," said his dad, who was breathing heavily from what should have been simple exertion, "looks like you found your first hobby." He took his son from his wife and put Scott back on the floor. Scott found the spring again.

Addison's voice turned ugly, even as the Sproing, Sproing, Sproing grew louder. "My child will not spend his time on the floor staring at the wall!"

"He's my son too you know," answered Stanley Junior. "Look, it's harmless fun. What's he going to do, eat the doorstop?"

"You think it's funny? How is that funny?" Scott's mother turned to face her husband and they both turned away from Scott.

"Addison, please, what did I do?"

"Nothing is what. You don't care about what I think!"

"But this is simple fun. I don't understand—"

"You're not the one who has to do the laundry!"

Stanley shook his head. "He's wearing a diaper. What's the deal?"

"Are you mocking me?"

"What? No. Addison, what do you want?" He breathed deeply and began to move toward the nearest chair. This seemed to be happening more and more. On the job site, his energy would flag and he would have to stop, sit down, and breathe. He would come home and immediately fall asleep in his chair.

Addison watched him in anger. "You're going to walk away? What is wrong with you? It is Saturday. We should be out doing stuff, but you just want to sleep. Am I not good enough for you?"

Stanley Junior thought before he answered. When he did, there was sadness in his eyes. "No, Addy—"

"Don't call me that!"

"Addison... No, I'm not sure it's me who's good enough for you. Honestly, Addison, you seem to hate everything. "This house is too small and too crowded and too much work. You don't like my job. It doesn't pay enough... I just do not see you happy."

"I have a child to worry about. Do I have to worry about you too?"

"I can take care of myself. You wanted a kid. There's only so much time in the day."

"What are you saying, that I don't do my share?"

There was plenty Stanley wished to say, but he had already said too much. Finally, he said, "Sometimes I wonder if you wanted the extra burden of a kid."

Addison went on the defensive. Sounds of Sproing, Sproing, Sproing accentuated her rant. "Sure, I wanted a kid! And he is not a kid; he is a child and he will be important, and he will become someone, and that won't happen in dirty ragged clothes on a dirty carpet staring at the wall."

Scott had begun to cry; the doorstop went silent. While his parents would easily assume it was from the need for a diaper change or from hunger, deep within, Scott knew better, although he would not be able to put it into words. Something was wrong and it always seemed to center on him.

Scott's mother and father looked at each other, unable to find the right words. Father wearily picked up son and moved slowly down the stairs. He stopped halfway to breathe again. He wondered if it was time to see a doctor. He also wondered where they would get the money.

Tucking the newest Schyler more securely to his chest, he grabbed the handrail, descended the remainder of the steps, and headed for the nearest chair. Mostly, he wanted someone to acknowledge him and appreciate all he tried to do. "I could use a little help," he whispered, as if in prayer.

"Are you alright?" Scott's mother called after her husband without making any move to go and see; her tone was more shrug than concern.

When she had finally gone downstairs, Addison had found Stanley asleep. Scott, now diaper less and in a wet mess, was sitting by the front door at a new doorstop. He happily Sproinged away. Scott had discovered a pattern.

"Damn it!" Addison cried, waking her husband. "This is the best you got?"

Stanley Junior struggled awake. He fluttered his eyes open and tried to focus. "I... I'm not feelin' so good," he said.

She smashed at him, "So, talk to somebody."

"I will!" Stanley stood angrily, took a deep breath, and stepped toward his son. "I'll take him!" he demanded.

Scott's mother backed away as her husband grabbed the diaper-bag, changed Scott, and dressed him. Not another word was said as father and son, with all the paraphernalia necessary for a two-year-old, walked out of the apartment.

The ever-angry voice followed them. "Sure, go to your mother's, you chicken... Her voice faded as the car roared away, and, as she would for years to come, Scott's mother stood in solitary silence and wondered why she was so alone.

ON THAT SAME DAY, in Grandma Ray's kitchen, Scott moved up a notch, from doorstop Sproing to cabinet door Click. As his dad settled in for an uninterrupted nap, and grandfather worked in the shop, Scott, under the watchful eyes of his grandma, was back on the floor, crawling mostly, but also attempting to stand. With the help of chairs and people's legs and anything within reach, he stepped and stretched on tiptoe to try to reach ever higher. He was no dummy. He knew where those peanut butter cookies were, even if he could not say "peanut butter" or reach them yet.

As he tried again for the countertop, his tiny legs

tired and he slumped. His little hands grabbed for the door pull on one of the old, painted, metal cabinets. Grandpa had felt no need to upgrade; they remained extremely functional after all. The door opened with a solid Click, startling Scott as it swung wide and almost carrying him with it. Grandma laughed, picked the boy up and, with another metallic, resounding Click, she closed the door. She handed Scott a cookie and stood him back up against the counter.

Instead of eating the cookie, however, Scott zoned in on the cabinet door. This time, he tried to open it. He tugged, wobbled, and tugged, then he sat down. He reached up and tugged again, harder this time. The door opened with a satisfying Click that nearly smacked him in the face, but it didn't. Scott giggled and then pushed the door closed. Click, again. Here was the pattern: Open, Click, Giggle. Close, Click, Giggle. Cookie, Giggle, Open, Click...

Stanley Schyler Junior entered the kitchen with a yawn and a big smile as he viewed the actions of his son.

"Did you have a nice nap?" his mother asked.

"Yeah, but it sure seems I'm sleeping a lot lately. I just don't have a lot of energy."

"Well, maybe you should see a doctor," she said while pouring him a cup of coffee. "You are your father's son, you know."

"It's not my heart." He paused to think about that. "Yeah, maybe..." he replied. He looked at his son. "You know, Scott was doing sort of the same thing at the house. I guess that's how kids learn, huh?" He told her about Scott's discovery of what he called *The Sproingy-Thingy.*

"That's so cute!" She smiled while watching another Click, Giggle. "I am worried he might catch his fingers. That would change his tune."

Scott's dad shrugged. "He's doing so far so good. I guess if he catches his fingers, he'll learn how not to."

"You sound just like your father. He's a bit young for a lesson, don't you think?"

"You started him!" he said. "I don't know, seems like he's figured it out pretty well so far!"

Open, Click, Giggle...

The back door opened with a start. Grandpa stood for a moment, breathing deeply. He was, as usual, sawdust loaded and tracking it in.

"Stanley," Grandma said, "can't you at least brush yourself off?"

Close, Click, Giggle...

"Yes, Dear." Stanley Senior smiled. It was standard conversation upon his reentering the house, and it had become a game between the two.

Open, Click, Giggle...

Stanley Senior eyed the two-year-old at the cabinet. "Hey," he said with a chuckle, "his mom's right, 'smarter than the average bear,' I see!"

"Yes, Dad," moaned the younger Stanley. How many times had he heard that? But he continued the thought. *How do I help Scott become that? How do I create with Addison what my mom and dad have? Is that even possible?* All this self-questioning was a dubious "gift" that he would pass to his son.

"Isn't he gonna smash his fingers?" Grandpa Stanley wondered. Then he asked, "Where *is* his mom?"

Close, Click, Giggle...

"She stayed home," said Stanley Junior, sighing deeply, "she, ah, wasn't feeling well."

The eyes of Scott's grandparents met in understanding. Grandpa Stanley said, "I'm not sure you are either."

"Look who's talking!" said son to father. "I'll go to the doctor if you go to the doctor!"

Stanley Senior answered, "There's nothing wrong with me a little less good cookin' won't fix." He playfully reached for his wife. "And a little more lovin'."

"Oh, stop," replied his wife, but she leaned into him.

Click, Giggle, Click, Giggle, Click—SMASH. Scott let out a wail as the inevitable occurred.

Grandma un-hugged Grandpa and dashed to Scott where she picked him up and said, "Come on, Little Bear, you've got plenty of time to learn. Now let's get you down for a nap... Ooh." She had placed her hand on a very soggy behind. "Maybe when you wake up, we'll try some new safer sounds."

Scott put his head on her shoulder in contented silence, and he was out like a light. Grandma Ray took him to the bedroom. Grandpa Stanley looked to his son. "That's a great kid, Stanley!"

"I'm learning," Stanley Junior said. "And so is Addison..."

AS THEIR GRANDSON NAPPED, Grandma Ray had walked to the garage to ask a small favor of her husband.

"You want me to carve you some ear plugs too?" Stanley Senior had replied when he had heard her idea. "I'll just have to stay in the shop longer."

"What's that?" asked Grandma Ray as she spied a new project.

"Oh, I have a client who wants an oak squirrel. Sort of ironic, huh? Oak, acorn, squirrel. Get it?"

"Yes, dear."

"I'll have to put the otter on hold. He kissed his wife on the forehead and asked, "Where'd Slim go?"

"They're going to try to work things out. We've got Scott for a couple days."

"Oh..." Stanley nodded. He crossed himself haphazardly and looked up to the heavens.

"Uh-huh," Grandma agreed. She closed the door as her husband continued to work.

WHEN GRANDMA RAY RETURNED to the crib in the guestroom, Scott was standing and peering, with hazy eyes, over the crib railing. "Daddy?" he asked.

"Not yet, Little Bear," said Grandma Ray as she reached for him and checked his diaper. "Daddy went home to talk to your mom. It's just you and me." She lifted him out of the crib and helped him wobble-walk down the hall. Once back to the kitchen, she said, "Hey, I have an idea. Do you want to try something?"

Scott nodded.

There on the kitchen linoleum, which Scott's father had helped his grandpa install, was a small assortment of pots and pans turned upside down. As his grandma placed Scott among them, he immediately picked up a pan and began slamming it to the floor.

Grandma Ray reached to the counter. She picked up two roughly rounded pieces of wood fresh from the shop, each one about five inches long, but they were well-sanded and splinter-free. "Let's try these instead," she said. She squatted down beside him and used one of the sticks to tap on a large Dutch Oven. Scott giggled and grabbed for the stick. As Grandma Ray gave it to him, he immediately poked her with it.

Grandma took it back. "No, this is a tool. It's a drumstick. Can you say drumstick?"

"Umstich," said Scott.

"Close enough for today. Try again." She showed him again—Tap, Tap, Tap. She gave him back the stick. Scott smiled and hit the biggest pan with the stick. It was a glancing blow, kind of a Thornk, but it resonated through the underside of the pan and Scott cheered.

"Now, you're getting it!" cried Grandma. "Try again!"

Thornk became a clear baritone peal as Scott found the center of the pan.

"Try another pan," said Grandma. She moved his hand to the smallest pot. This one was an old, dented, aluminum, tea kettle, and the tone climbed the musical scale. It was mostly a dull Tink, but it was different than Thornk and Click and Sproing. Scott tittered and hit the kettle again and again.

Not sure how the two-fisted technique would work, Grandma just laid down the second mini-drumstick next to him. It took Scott a couple of minutes to see it. When he did, he stopped, curled his left paw around the second stick and took off like a frisky pony kicking its heels on a crisp spring morning. It was no Phil Collins drumming *In the Air Tonight*, but it was an inquisitive two-year-old little boy proving an ear for rhythm and pattern. It was a mess of sounds that only a grandmother could love, and it only lasted for about three minutes, but during that time, Scott and Grandma beamed from ear to ear.

After a time, Scott let out a sigh, tired but satisfied. He dropped the sticks to the floor near the tea kettle and crawled over to the back door. He looked around, found what he was looking for, and he went back to where it had started. The Sproing, Sproing, Sproing of the doorstop was comfortable to the little musician, and he turned drowsy. On the floor in his Grandma's kitchen, he fell asleep with his finger on the doorstop.

When Grandpa came in, Grandma "shushed" him. He stepped over Scott and let him be. "Concert over?" he whispered.

"I think it's just beginning," she replied.

WHEN ADDISON AND STANLEY came to retrieve Scott, they appeared, to the grandparents, to be in good spirits. Grandma Ray asked, "Did you have a good mini-vacation?"

Stanley Junior said, "It was very relaxing. We got some things sorted out."

Addison added, "It is nice sometimes to not have a kid, er child, to deal with. Where is he, I want to see my, er, *our* son."

"He's in the basement. I put him there for all our sanity," Grandma Ray joked.

Addison did not see the humor. "The basement?" She charged through the kitchen to the stairwell and climbed down.

"It's okay... Grandpa's down there with him!" Grandma Ray looked at Stanley Junior and they followed Addison.

Scott's mother stood at the bottom of the stairs staring at her son with a mixture of anger and disbelief. Her son was pounding his pots and pans on the hard concrete floor of the laundry room, away from foot traffic. Grandpa Stanley sat nearby with earphones in against the "music". He was reading a book.

What might have been a hint of amusement shown in Addison's lip curl, but it did not make it to her eyes. Her proud form would not allow her to bend to whimsy. "How do you stand this racket?" she yelled.

Neither Scott nor Grandpa had heard her come down the stairs; they both looked up at once.

Addison pulled Scott from his "drums." He held the two sticks firmly. He looked at his mother with a smile, but she did not smile back. "On the concrete? What if he cracks his head? Some babysitters you are!"

"Addison, we're not baby-sitters. We're his grandparents. He has a knack for beats and sounds," said Grandma, "and it seems to calm him down. We're watching him."

Grandpa Stanley wryly nodded to whatever his wife had just said.

Scott began to rock in his mother's arms, bobbing his head back and forth on her chest. She gripped the top of his head to get him to stop. "He's not the one that needs to be calm!"

Every person in the room knew to let that remark die.

Grandpa Stanley removed his headset, cleared his throat, and attempted to explain. "He has a lot of nervous energy. The drumming seems like it focuses that energy. Since he found the doorstop, he has not stopped wanting to hear the beat. I think if he had a real drum set, we'd have a prodigy on our hands. You should watch him work!"

Addison took the mini-sticks from her boy and threw them on the floor near the pans. Then she went on the attack. "There are no prodigies at two. Great musicians are one in a million. Even then some of them don't get a break."

Stanley Junior looked at her and then looked away. He thought she was speaking about herself, and he wondered why she didn't do anything about it.

Grandma Stanley picked up the sticks. She held them out to Addison. "Little Bear has a lot of fun with these; he's amazing to watch—"

"Little pain in the butt, more like," Addison said. Now holding Scott as if he were plunder from a hard-fought battle, she gathered the diaper and toy bags. She took the sticks from Grandma Ray and laid them on the dryer. She scowled when Scott reached for them. "These toys," she said with disdain, "will stay here."

Scott started to cry, but his mother would not be deterred. She brushed past her husband and stomped back up the stairs. The three remaining adults looked at each other uneasily. Grandma Ray said, "You know Stanley, you're always welcome here."

"I know Mom," he sighed. "Thanks for trying with Scott." He wearily trod up the basement steps.

IN THE COMING YEARS, Scott would find his own tools. Whether wooden spoons on pots and pans he would grab from the kitchen, or bottles pulled from the pantry, or pencils and pens, or most anything within reach, Scott would create his own music. His interest in drums did not, like many hobbies, falter over time. He listened and observed. He watched drummers on

TV and YouTube. He begged his mother for a drum set. As *if!*

As time went by, and the tensions between mother and son grew, now without Dad, she would take away the tools. He would find more. Fingernails worked if there was nothing else available, nervous ticking from finger to finger a clue to the restless energy inside him. His mother was embarrassed for him and avoided the subject all together.

While Addison denied him, his grandparents had seen something in him. When Scott turned eleven, just after he had finished his fourth wooden animal figure, his grandparents had, for Christmas that year, bought him a junior drum-kit. It was a simple Walmart set: bass, snare, and symbol, but it was a start. The kit replaced the pots and pans in their basement. Scott knew he was welcome to come practice anytime.

"He's an amazing thing to watch," Grandpa Stanley would tell people, including Scott's mother, if he could get in an encouraging word. "Your not-so-little-any-more, smarter than the average bear is really getting this. You should see how precise he is with his timing and technique."

Addison was not to be swayed. "He's eleven, for God sakes!"

Even as Scott held on to drums and lessons and practice, his mother told him it was—*he was* —worthless. "It's all so much noise! What idiot told you you could play the drums?" Scott wondered what had happened to make his mother so cold.

After particularly brutal battles with her, and if his grandparents were not available, he would resort to closing the door to his room. He would attempt to drown out the dissonance of his mother. He would, while putting his head against the wall, question his abilities in all things to the sounds of Thud, Thud, Thud.

7 | Of Oboes and Ogres

THE SWARM OF BODIES buzzing to the Euclid band room came to an abrupt halt. One of the double doors was locked. Forty-three want-to-be musicians (or more realistically, students whose parents wished them to play an instrument), and one new taller-than-most kid, wearing glasses and with drumsticks sticking out of his back pocket, were attempting to squeeze through the only opening door at the same time. Rodney had stepped through and stopped to assess the situation. Scott and those behind him smashed forward like falling dominoes. Behind him, whirled shouts of, "Hey, Stupid" mingled with, "Move!" Scott felt accusatory eyes upon him, and he wished to shrink.

Rodney looked around. "I don't see Ogre anywhere," he said.

The Concert/Marching/Jazz band director's real name was Ogden, but the students had other ideas about the type of person he was. "He's usually in his office and comes out when he feels like it," said Rodney, then he walked away to the instrument racks.

Scott was lost and looking for his place. He paused and adjusted his glasses, as if that would help him know what to do. What he saw was the same band room frenzy he had become accustomed to.

There was much stereotypicality in Scott's new band. From school to school, the sections placed on the wide tiers of the stage were all the same. There were the shy, *but often cute,* female flutists in the front row. Clarinetists sat next to them, all of whom, Scott thought, wished to be saxophonists instead. It was the sexier of the reed instruments, but was not, according to his mother, "a 'real' orchestral instrument," it was meant more for bars and that "low-life jazz stuff."

Behind the reeds were what Scott called the Brass Asses, loud and noisy, constantly tooting the trumpets and occasional trombone. They included the mandatory lone sousaphonist who never seemed to have enough breath for the low notes.

This section was where Rodney was headed. He carried his own "bone," but he was using his mouth as its replacement, moving up and down the scale in fourteen-year-old baritone, "Bouu-wough, bou-wee-bough." Rodney's empty arm pantomimed the trombone slide as his voice found the pitches, "Broowough" to the south, arm outstretched, then, "Brieeie," elbow bent to the north and then down again. *How does his mom stand that kid?*

Behind the Brass Asses were the percussion section, a totally different beast, and a group that Scott was not always proud to be a part of. There were the bells, gongs and tympani, bass drums and snares, all of which were supposed to be individual parts working toward whatever thematic sound was necessary for the symphonic unity of the Euclid High School Band.

But the raucous noises and careless, disorganized pummeling and pounding of the various drums could, at times, be near painful to him. The drummers were seldom anything near his mother's, or even his grandparents', standard of "professional."

Upon giving him his drum-kit a few years back, his grandparents had given him a lesson he had heard before: "This is a tool. You have an interest in learning? Then do it right."

At home, he would YouTube the Buddy Riches and Neal Pearts of the world, and he quietly and quickly learned the rudiments. These were the basics. He discovered how to hold the sticks and to use them for a hundred different sounds and accents: single and double stroke rolls, paradiddles, up-strokes, and rebound strokes and flams. He realized it was much more than just beating on some pots and pans.

What attracted Scott most was the *drum groove*—the mathematically precise usage of those various stick techniques to make an interesting sound while keeping perfect time. Without a steady beat, a band has no chance to sound good. With only a beat, the band sounds boring. The lead singer might be the showboat, the one saying, "I'm here," but that lead singer cannot survive without the beat. It is the meter of poetry; it is life's ancient pulse emanating from deep within the soul.

This was becoming the heartbeat of Scott's life. He lived for it, even when it turned to throbbing anger.

What he could not understand was the hatred of his

mother toward this new-found passion. She was, she said, a musician. She must have worked around, and understood the need for, drummers, but his practicing, on practice pad or drum-kit, would set her voice to clanging like a dented cymbal at the thought that "all that racket" was worth anything. "You just love giving your mother a headache, don't you?"

"Yeah, Mother," he would retort. But he kept at it. He learned on his own. His desire for proficiency on the drums only grew, so he practiced. No, really. Not like being forced to play the flute because your parents had, but because he wanted to. As he had tried to explain to Miss Walters, it was the one thing he just knew he was good at. But this was tempered by the thought that he would never be any better than what his mother told him he was.

Scott climbed the risers toward the drummers, some of whom looked at him quizzically. Most ignored him as he did them. He chose a seat against the wall behind the tympani and minded his own business. He sat, stretched his legs, and folded his drumsticks across his chest. He waited, wishing to prove his worth as a competent percussionist.

The bell rang. Scott watched Rodney take his seat a couple of rows away and to his left. He heard him continue to bleat, "Wahah-Wahah," now on his actual instrument. Scott further scanned the room, and his eyes landed on those of Sarah, seated center front row. She saw him and swiftly turned away.

He glanced again. *Oh, God. She's one of those.* She had

not one, but three instruments, in metal stands no less, by her chair: clarinet, oboe and, standing larger than the girl herself, a bassoon. *Who the heck plays a bassoon?*

So, there were two options. One: she was a band nerd. She had shown some talent, and the director needed her to try different instruments for the various pieces they were working on; she wanted to get the "A", so she did what she was told. Two: she was a musician, one who appreciated and practiced the art. This was a term he was still wrapping his head around. All he did was smack little sticks onto tightly strung leather and plastic circles. *Is that music? Is that art?* Art is carving birds and animals, creating something from nothing. His grandfather was an artist.

So, which was Sarah? Band nerd or artist? He found himself really wanting to find out, but he dropped his head to his chest in defeat as his brain pounded the reality. He was not good enough. *No way. No way. No way.*

The band room went quiet, at least as quiet as a high school band can become. Scott turned his head toward the center of the room where a tall student, even taller than Scott's five-eleven, had picked up a pen and clip board off the worn, wooden podium. He wore a Euclid baseball cap and facial hair. Hair, in its many forms and placements, was a badge of honor, a sign of achievement; obviously, here was a junior or a senior. The tall one commanded the room as he scanned the faces to take attendance. He knew most of the kids and only called a name if that student was not there. He stopped on: Barkley, Benjamin. "Ben, are you here?"

"He's sick," called out Rodney. *Of course, Rodney would know!*

The tall one marked the sheet and then continued, "Peterson? Peterson? Anthony?"

As if on cue, Anthony Peterson clanged the band room door open. "Sorry, Eric!" The blond boy, with wispy fly-a-way hair and carrying no books, back-pack, or instrument, headed up the tiers. He stopped along the way to high-five and say "sup" to everyone. He casually strolled through the music stands, and he eventually found a seat next to Scott. *Figures!* The two boys glanced at each other but that was all.

Eric—now Scott had a name anyway—gave Anthony the evil eye. Anthony just smiled as if the whole world should be pleased that he had arrived, late or not. Apparently, this was a regular occurrence.

Eric stopped in his list again as a balding, wrin-kly-suited, old guy stepped from out of the band office and stood next to him. He was no taller than, and every bit as worn as, the podium that he stood next to. Eric leaned toward him. "Hello, Mr. Ogden. Here is a new name: Skyler? Scott Skyler? Scott, are you here?"

Every eye in the place pivoted to the back of the band. Mr. Ogden's gaze followed the students. "Great!" growled Mr. Ogden, impolitely loud enough for all to hear, "all I need is another percussionist. We don't need no more cowbell." He laughed at his own joke and repeated it, "More cowbell," a reference to some long-lost movie. His students were oblivious and stared at the director. Many just kept on talking.

Scott's face turned blank, in part due to the mispronunciation of his name but also due to the attitude of the teacher. He opted to move his sticks to his back pocket. He had no wish to be "noticed" on his first day.

He was not. Mr. Ogden barely even looked to Scott. "Move on, Eric," he said.

Eric too, barely looked Scott's way, and he continued through the roster, ending on the Vees: Vaughn. "Hi, Sarah." Eric's eyes lit up; his smile lingered on the triple-threat instrumentalist. She returned a little wave.

Really? Scott crossed his now drumstick-empty arms. *That figures too.* His hopes, what few there had been, were now dashed. He reminded himself of who he was.

"Warmups please, Mr. Sanchez," barked Mr. Ogden. "Warm-ups. Let's go!"

"Sarah, do your oboe thing please," said Eric.

Scott saw her in profile three rows down and watched her every move. Sarah already had her instrument to her lips, attempting to keep the reed moist. Her smallish, pretty hands (as Scott compared them to his) found the correct fingering, took a breath, and Scott's too. She completed a perfect orchestral "A".

From there, Eric directed the group up and down a couple of scales. The snare drummers in Scott's row stood and created the correct cadences. Scott stood with them, but, unsure of what to play, he stood politely at attention and mimicked their movements.

Mr. Ogden stood behind Eric scanning the room. His eyes lit on the new kid in the back, but his voice pounced on the student next to him, "Mr. Peterson... Mr. Peterson!"

A startled Peterson, who had been screwing and unscrewing the strap of a cymbal looked up and blurted, "What?!"

"That cymbal..." Mr. Ogden's tone was menacing, "...that cymbal is worth more than you are, Peterson. What should you be doing at this second?"

"Well, I..."

"Never mind... Never mind! Go find the new guy the proper music. Get him a folder. Show him where a practice room is." He sternly pointed a pudgy hand toward a hallway. "Take him and you and your snare there, and both of you practice." His words were an echo, "Practice, practice." He shook his head in disbelief at student stupidity.

From across the room, a trombone raspberry bellowed. "Wah-Wah-Wahh." The band tittered. A drummer to Scott's far left answered with a rim-shot.

"Cut the... Cut the crap!" shouted Mr. Ogden. Scott was discovering how the band director had gotten the name Ogre. All around him it went silent. The crap was cut.

"C'mon," said Anthony. He picked up his snare and was already half-way across the room. Scott apprehensively stood to follow. His tall frame, balancing on Frankenshoes, cautiously maneuvered through the seats so as not to find someone's toes. The shortest distance out of the instrument and music stand maze seemed to be straight down, past his bassoon player.

He stepped lightly, but his mega-feet could not avoid the bassoon stand nor the four-thousand-dollar instrument that rested on it. Sarah let out a gasp. Scott mouthed, "Shit." He attempted to stop both the bassoon and his large body from crumpling to the floor.

There was simply not enough room for girl, instruments, and Scott. As he struggled to save everything, he felt and heard two music stands teeter and fall behind him. Scott blushed; his heart beat faster. Someone, amidst all the hoots and hollering, announced the expected, "Way to go, Slim!"

The room exploded, and the band director didn't help the situation. "Ya walk much?" Mr. Ogden asked. "Pick up your feet." He stared at Scott. "C'mon, pick 'em up!"

Scott put his head down, and he cursed his Frankenshoes. His audience presented a variety of responses, some nervous, some concerned, but too many were jubilant at the plight of the new guy.

Fortunately, Sarah had caught the large woodwind, but she would not look at Scott. Rodney, who's music stand was one that had toppled, picked it up; he was replacing all the music that had fluttered to the ground. He stopped and looked at Scott. "It's okay, Sli... Sorry, Dude. It's gotta get better. Right?"

Scott shuffled on. *Yep! Meet the new kid!*

Mr. Ogden pulled the class back together. "Wilson's *Frosted Fanfare March*. Get it out. Get it out. Now!" His old-guy fuse was preparing to blow. "Eric, take them through this. I want it clear, clear and in unison and at the correct tempo, or I'll find another teacher's aide." He stormed into the office, leaving the door ajar so he could hear.

"Uh... Yes, sir," was all Eric could reply. "Okay guys, let's settle down and do this." He looked at Sarah and quietly asked, "Are you okay?"

Flustered, she whispered, "Yes," then she looked around her chair to resettle her belongings. On the floor between her legs she found a worn drumstick with the initials S.S.S.S. neatly carved into the end of it. She picked it up, fingered the lettering, and looked after Scott to see if she could get it to him, but he was gone. To follow would bring the wrath of Mr. Ogden. Plus, Eric had begun the count...

She placed the drumstick in her backpack.

"...*Frosted Fanfare March*. Let's do this right. One, two, three, four. One, two..."

Down the hall, Scott entered an eight-foot-square piano practice room, barely larger than he was. Anthony sat in the only chair; his feet propped up on the piano as if he owned it. He rocked the chair on its hind legs. Phone in hand, his fingers flew as he texted with someone. He tittered at what he viewed on his screen. As Scott shut the door, Anthony announced with glee, "You must be Honeybunch!"

Scott froze. *Was this to be Steve Martin 2.0? Social media is such a wonderful thing!* His first reaction was to grab this clown and fold him under the piano. Instead, remembering what he was attempting: to speak not at all unless it was absolutely necessary, he simply scowled at Anthony, who was shorter, and maybe stupider, than he. *How could that be? We both ended up in the same room!*

Scott stood at the piano bench looking for his music, but he saw nothing. He didn't want to ask; that would be conversation, but he felt he had to. "Music?"

"Who needs music?" asked Anthony. "You think I was going to practice anyway?"

Scott answered, "So what's your deal?" He was learning that most jerks and bullies were looking for an audience; if you got them alone, they were not so bad.

"Whaddya mean?" asked Anthony.

"I mean... So, why are you in band then?"

"What's it to you, Honeybunch?"

Scott took one step. He hovered over the seated boy and his already tipping chair. He pressed forward just enough to force Anthony to move his feet so he would not fall backward. Anthony's phone slipped from his hand and clattered to the linoleum. He shrank into his chair while Scott clenched and unclenched his fists, deciding what to do.

Scott's first choice was to tear this kid and the room apart. That would not be good. He leaned menacingly into Anthony and decided he would just ask a question; "Are you always a jerk, or just with new kids?"

Anthony's only answer was a frightened, "Huh?"

"So far, I've only seen jerk."

Anthony looked from his phone on the floor to Scott towering above him. He was discovering things he had not known about Honeybunch. He tried to start over.

"I... I like the drums."

Scott relaxed and stepped away from Anthony. "So, show me something,"

"I forgot my sticks."

"Uh-huh," said Scott.

"I did," Anthony whined. "You sound like Mr. Ogre."

"Are you always in trouble?" asked Scott.

Anthony shrugged. "Ehh..." He looked warily at the bigger boy but, deciding the danger had passed, he reached for his phone and leaned back in the chair again.

Scott sighed. "If you're not going to practice, I'd like to."

"Have at it." Anthony slid the snare toward Scott.

"Music?" Scott asked again, as he adjusted the snare in front of him. He began to reach for his drumsticks.

"You don't need music, Honeybun—" Anthony thought better of using the nickname, especially when he saw Scott reach around to his back pocket. When he realized it was a harmless move, he shrugged again and went back to his phone. Social media: this was Anthony's survival plan.

Scott felt his right back pocket and pulled out... one drumstick. Now he was puzzled. He felt his other back pocket. Somehow, somewhere, he had lost a drumstick. He looked on the floor. He looked around Anthony's chair and under the piano bench. He opened the door and looked back down the hall. Music blasted from the band room, but he saw no stick. He closed the door. Obviously, there would be no practice, at least not on a real drum.

He looked at the S.S.S.S. carved into the remaining stick. *It's tough to be competent and professional with only one stick!*

He looked at his practice partner. There was no help. Scott decided he would play anyway. He would use some of the things his grandfather had taught him when he started to carve. He could hear the music in his head; he could visualize the strokes on his virtual drum.

He sat on the piano bench, his back against the piano keys, and he practiced his technique, drumstick in one hand—air-drumming—really. Anthony gave him a strange look, but he did not speak.

After a while, Scott stopped. He looked at Anthony, and then he opened his backpack to pull out his Triceratops. Anthony could think whatever he wanted about that. He could not know all the hard work that had gone into it. He would not care that since the first carving, Scott had filled out a good Jurassic Park's worth of wooden dinosaurs, each, Scott felt, better than the last.

As he had moved from place to place, following the whims of his mother, at least he had kept up with the carving. His grandpa had helped him from afar, sometimes by phone, and even sometimes via Skype, but it was not the same as being there in person. He was glad to be home for that!

He was ready to try something new, but he was not sure what. His grandfather would ask him what was it he cared about. Was it people? Was it animals, or was it things? What did he care enough about to whittle? Grandpa Stanley had mentioned flowers for his mom, for example, but that was a non-starter. His skill level was increasing, but his ideas of what to carve were at a standstill. *Maybe a drumstick? Ha ha!*

He went back to air-drumming with intent. If you had looked in the room, you would have thought there was a real drum kit there. The piano bench became the drum throne; Scott surrounded the actual snare with virtual kick-drum, tom-tom, and cymbals and, with only one stick, Scott started to make music.

Across the tiny room, Anthony Peterson slowed his texting, grinned in derision at first and then began to really observe. Scott continued to "play" with intensity, while Anthony's scorn changed to fascination.

When the bell rang, they packed up to go. Scott picked up the drum to take it back to the band room. Something had changed. The boys didn't speak; they didn't slap backs, do high-fives or become best buds. However, Anthony did offer a small wave, and he told himself he would have to find this guy his music.

8 | ROUTE 7–B

SCOTT SCHYLER'S FIRST THOUGHT upon hearing the last bell of his first day at Euclid High was that at least he had survived. Then he realized he had found no one to tell him where to catch the bus. Four miles was a long way to walk and there was no way he would call his mother to pick him up. As he walked to the main office, he dodged students and reviewed the day with much sarcasm. *Well, let's see... I had a nice welcome from comedian Steve Martin. I found out the band teacher is a real ogre. Hmm, what else? I kicked at, glared at, and eventually fell over, a girl who seems nice and cute, and will never know I exist.*

Survival, Scott thought, as he opened the door to the main office, was about all he could hope for. He had survived science, algebra, and American History without too much pain. He had eaten alone at lunch. He had not seen the girl, Sarah, but he remembered her with a mixture of sweet and sour. Neither had he seen that other kooky kid, Rodney. *Probably different schedules.*

As the day progressed, the attitude from students had improved. Apparently, the media wonder of SlimScottScrawny was limited to a few, and the new kid novelty was wearing off. *Whew!*

"Route 7–B," said the office lady, after Scott told her his address. "Follow the maddening hordes to the buses," she said, "it'll be marked on the side of the bus."

"7–B," he repeated, as he reached again for the main door, only to have it opened by the tall upperclassman from band. *Eric, was it?*

Eric stepped aside and with a sweep of—come on through—he motioned for Scott to pass before he did. "Hey," he said, "welcome to Euclid and welcome to band. I'm sorry you had such a rough introduction. Do you play drums well?"

Scott was stunned. He had thought Eric had not even seen him. That would have been easier to handle. "Um, yeah, pretty good."

Eric continued to smile but asked, "Does that mean you try, or does that mean you just like to screw around?" Eric had had his fill of drummer wannabes too.

Scott went on the defensive. "If someone had let me play, you might have found out. What does it matter to you anyway?"

Eric stepped out of the way as other students were trying to enter the office. "Excuse me," he said to them. He grabbed Scott by the shoulder and tugged him out of the stream. "Nothin' really. I'd like to hear you play. It's just that I'm sort of a band geek. I'd like us to be good, but we have a lot going against us."

"I could tell," said Scott, "but what does it matter?"

Eric thought. "I like to be good. You may have noticed that there are expectations in the band room, but people don't really try to meet them, even when they talk about it."

Yeah, even the director...

Eric asked, "Are you a freshman?"

"Yeah, why?"

"'Cause a ninth grader usually doesn't care. They come in thinking they own the school and that they won't have to work. You sound different, but you got booted from the room."

"Not my fault," Scott said tersely. "I'm gonna miss my bus." He moved to pass Eric, but the bigger boy stopped him again.

"No... No, I know it wasn't your fault, but you could have said something—"

"I shouldn't have had to."

"But if you don't speak, nobody knows who you are."

"I like it that way!" Scott shoved past Eric.

Eric was not so sure. "Okay... See you tomorrow."

Scott Schyler stormed outside to the bus lanes and worked his way through throngs of students, all of whom seemed to be attempting to speak to someone fifty yards away. "Hey, watch it," some said, as he barreled past them without looking up. The noise was brutal, and his heart began to pump faster in apprehension. *Damn that Eric!* Just because school was over did not mean the day's trauma was. *Why can't people see me for the good?* Then: *Is there any good?*

He trudged along the row of busses until he found his: 7–B, dirty yellow, and mostly full already. That was not good at all. Getting on a new bus was near the lowest level of hell. He had, thankfully, avoided the lowest level, that was first hour gym class, missed this morning because of his mother. *There's always tomorrow...*

The bus contained one scowling bus driver: an overweight woman with short hair and wearing a big puffy vest. She looked past retirement age, and she held the obligatory, gigantic, coffee cup in one hand and the door handle in the other. It was halfway shut, and Scott squeezed his way in.

"Are you on Seven–B?" asked the driver. His was a new face; she was supposed to ask.

 Scott adjusted his backpack, He wanted to respond with, "Would I be here if I wasn't supposed to be?" He thought better of it and just nodded.

She shut the door behind him. "You'll need to let me know when we get close," continued the driver.

He nodded again. At least he knew the streets.

The students were a mixture of underclass persons; most seniors drove. All on board were tired. He scanned the seats for an opening, hopefully private and away from people. This was the dilemma: if you did not get on first, or you were new, the good seats were gone, and you had to sit next to someone you despised, or who despised you.

Students were in the aisles trying to find seats, or seated and holding a seat for a friend, or sprawled across the whole seat so they did not have to share. Scott was trying to think. He looked in his backpack again to be sure he still had his remaining drumstick. He had looked all over for the second one. He went back to the band room at lunch, but it had been locked; he looked for students who may have been in band, to no avail, and even went to Lost and Found, but no luck there either. There were other stick sets at home, but this was his first good pair and a part of who he was.

He looked up again to find a space. About halfway down and on the left, he spotted Sarah seated next to the girl he had seen her with at the lockers. He ducked his head, attempting to avoid that section. He moved with the flow about four seats back and got stopped again.

In this fishbowl, numerous eyes perceived a new face and some wondered, out loud and often rudely, if this was the place he should be. "Hey, you, you're not on this bus!" shouted one *gentleman* in the back, the logic-fault of the comment again not lost on Scott. *I'm here aren't I?*

"Sup. New kid." came from another section of the bus, while someone who obviously had seen Steve Martin's tweet called out, "Look everybody, it's that Slim guy." Some looked; some tittered; some jeered. No one attempted to help or be kind. Scott blushed. He had nowhere to go.

"Maybe Cheri will let you sit on her lap!" yelled a nasty voice from the back.

"Shut-up!" This retort came from the front seat, voiced by an obviously more mature young lady and an incredibly involved student. Scott could tell by her real leather briefcase and how she seemed to be over-dressed for a job interview. "Leave him alone, you guys!"

The same nasty voice replied, "Screw you, Cheri, you just want to suck his..." This response was fortu-nately drowned out by the laughter of the passengers. The bus driver tried not to grin as she scanned the seats through the huge, interior, rear-view mirror. Obviously, Cheri's word meant much with this crowd.

By this time, most people were seated and anxious to be off. The bus would not move if all were not prepared. Scott was left standing in the middle of the bus. Each seat had someone or two someones in it, and it was easy to tell who of the singles would never budge, but somehow, he had to force a choice.

Sarah and her friend had been so busy chatting, they had not acknowledged the happenings around them, so Scott was surprised when Sarah made a motion to a smallish boy behind her to move over. The boy, who looked more like he was a sixth grader, was very small with braces and bad acne. He was hogging the whole seat with his backpack and playing with a Rubik's cube. The kid looked at Sarah, snarled weakly, noted the size of Scott, and moved the backpack into his lap. He continued turning the Rubik colors. Sarah turned back around with no discussion. Scott was relieved but cautious. He did not want to bump, kick, or do anything to draw even more attention.

The driver put the bus in gear, checked the side mirrors, and let out on the clutch; a cloud of diesel enveloped the bus and its occupants. The student noise was a dull roar competing with the sound of the engine. The bus bounced and jostled, but at least they were on their way.

In front of Scott, Sarah and the other girl had their noses in their laps looking at something and whispering. Nervously, he sank into the seat, glanced at Rubiks Boy, but he made no effort to talk to him. He watched street signs out the window.

Hi," Sarah said.

Scott jumped.

She had turned to face him—her whole head and body—so it was not an accident.

Now what? "Hi," Scott said back.

"This is my friend, Darla," Sarah said.

"Hi, Darla."

Darla giggled.

"That was neat what you did in English today," Sarah said.

"What?" That had been a long time ago and many embarrassments away.

"That thing about greatness. Nobody reads that way; it's like you're a speech master or something."

He sure would not be proving that now. "Th... Thanks," Scott stumbled from shock.

Sarah kept trying. "Had you read that before?"

"No."

"Um... Well, it was cool. Do you have it memorized yet?"

"We have to memorize?" asked Scott.

"Oh, yeah, you just got here. Yeah, Miss Walters likes us to get really deep into this literature stuff. I get stuck at the part about recognizing your potential and how resolute you have to be."

"Limited by how you choose, how you use your freedom, how resolute you are..." Scott emphasized the word resolute, and then he defined it: "How strong you are."

"What? Wait. You have it memorized?" Sarah was re-impressed.

Scott shied back into his seat. He didn't want to be too school-kiddish, but yeah, he could read well and picked up stuff—information—quickly. He took off his glasses because of a gigantic smudge and quickly demurred. "Well, sort of."

Sarah turned back around. All went quiet for a couple of blocks. The bus brakes squealed periodically as students got off; the interior of the bus became less noisy.

As the doors closed, Sarah spun around again. So, why the four esses?"

"What?"

"Four esses?" Sarah held up his drumstick and touching the S.S.S.S. inscription.

"Gimme that!" Scott reached for the stick.

Sarah pulled it back. "You could ask nice," she teased. "I looked for you all day, but I guess we don't have any other classes together. Silly? Strange? Slightly-Sneaky-Scott? That's your name isn't it? I'm not sure I know your last name. But four?"

Darla chimed in. "We saw today in the hall what not to call you!"

"Where'd you find it?" Scott asked, trying to ignore the taunts.

"Under my band chair, where you, uh, left it. Can you play, or do you just carry them to look cool?"

"Why does everyone ask the same thing?"

Sarah asked again, "Well, can you?"

"Can you play the bassoon?"

"Better than you can play the drums."

"You can't know that." Scott's patience waned. "Now give it back!"

Darla piped up. "Don't be mean!" She looked out the window as the bus slowed. To Sarah she said, "We're here."

The bus jerked to a stop. Both girls stood, grabbed their backpacks, and Sarah picked up her oboe case. Sarah playfully demanded again, "Tell me what S.S.S.S. means."

Scott was unsettled by the teasing. If this was playful, it was not something he had learned in his household. Were they just having fun, or were they wishing to be mean? He stuck out his hand.

"Girls, let's go!" said the bus driver impatiently. She had a schedule to keep.

"Tell me..." Sarah smiled, but she would not give in.

Scott frowned. "It should be obvious. Something Stupid Said Sarah." He knew he was rude the second the words sprang from his mouth.

"Fine. Here." Sarah said curtly. She handed him the stick and turned away with finality.

The two girls headed for the front of the bus and down the steps.

Scott felt like an idiot again. She could have thrown it away. He should be grateful. "Sarah, thank you!" he called. She did not look back. She may have not heard him, or she may have heard him and decided it was too late to expect politeness from this big jerk.

He glumly watched them walk away from the bus, then he reached into his backpack. He pulled out the first stick to compare the two; he needed to make sure they were again a team.

Rubiks Boy peered at the sticks and asked, "Do you play the drums?"

Scott rolled his eyes. *Ya think?* Sticks in hand, he began to rat-a-tat quietly on the seat—Sarah's seat—in front of him. The taps from his precious sticks soothing him, he drifted back to when he had received them, and wished he and his mother could communicate more like they had then.

SMYRNA, TENNESSEE HAD BEEN hot and humid. The town was small. The apartment his mother had rented was up three flights of stairs in an old building that had not seen paint on its clapboard walls since the Civil War. Late on their first night, they switched on the light after hearing noises, only to find roaches scattering to the four walls. Mother made them sleep in the car, and they went to look for a new place the next morning. The next apartment was not much better. What both had learned was the simple fact that there are more bugs, and stranger, in Tennessee than in Colorado. They would have to make do.

After his dad's death, Addison and he had struggled in the Englewood house for three years. Mother had sold it to pay bills, and they had survived in an apartment (and a different school), another year or so after that. Scott had barely survived middle school, with one exception. He had soared, like Moses, in math, even taking advanced classes. Something about that precision inside him. They kept busy. He saw his grandparents a lot, and that helped him some through the loss of his father. Addison, because she was working, also mellowed. It was only when they were idle that they had to consider their loss. The anger and guilt would return, as would the fighting.

Right before Scott would have enrolled at Euclid, one of his mother's friends had heard about "a great opportunity" in Smyrna, and she was moving. Perhaps because of wanderlust, or loneliness (*certainly not from any reasoning that included discussion with her son!*), they packed up the Hyundai and followed her. Addison's in-laws were eager to have them stay, but as usual, Addison would have her way.

Scott started high school far away from home. Tennessee schools were not as advanced, and he found himself becoming instantly bored. He was always in trouble for dozing off or for messing around in the back of the room. That was at the first school. It would get worse at the second.

After the first day of work, Scott knew his mother was having much the same reaction. "All I do," she would say, "is watch battery boxes being filled with acid all day long. Box and box and box and box. There must be a better way!"

She was usually tired and always cranky. Scott felt the same, but with the bonus that he had no drums. As usual, there had been no argument. Addison had put the hammer down. "We don't know where we will stay, we don't have room in the car. They'll have drums at school." The drum-kit, which he had been adding to with extra cymbals and better-quality drums, would have to stay in storage at Grandpa's.

Scott had wanted to be put into storage too, rather than go with her. He had made this abundantly clear with slamming doors and head banging, and lots of rebellious disappearing. He rode to his grandparent's every chance he got, where he would find calm, sanity, and his drums. There he would often spill his guts. "Can't I just stay here? She is so mean! I can't even take my drums. She doesn't care at all. Can't I just stay here? Please, Grandma? Please?" In this place, his words could tumble out in full torrent (and he sounded a little like his mother).

"Whoa!" said Grandma, "You can't just come barging in here wanting to move in, Scott. We love you, but you and your mom have to work this out."

"But Mother's always mad. She yells at me for nothing. Why do we have to move?"

Grandma Ray smiled as she attempted to explain, "Everybody fights, Slim. Forty years now for your Grandpa and me." She paused with recollections both sad and happy. She considered how deep to go with her grandson. "She's doing her best. Everybody always does their best, even when it might not seem that way to you. You and she will have to work things out. It's best if you just..." She wrapped her arms around his seated frame and, with moist eyes, looked through the open kitchen window. "You are always welcome here. I hope you guys do well, and I hope you come back. But that'll have to be when your mom figures out what she wants for you both.

Scott's voice rose in anger. "She doesn't think of us *both!*"

Grandma Ray shut him down. "It's how *you* act, Scott. You may not always like what is given to you, but you must learn to live through it and work out how to manage it. It's about your choices not your mothers."

ON THE BUS, SCOTT STOPPED drumming and gazed out the window. Then he made a connection, albeit unwillingly, "We are all free to choose our attitude." *Grandma and Koestenbaum could have been pals.*

The bus stopped again to let students off. Scott looked at the signs. He thought he might be getting close but no, not yet. The bus was emptying out rapidly. Only he, Rubiks Boy, and a couple of others, remained.

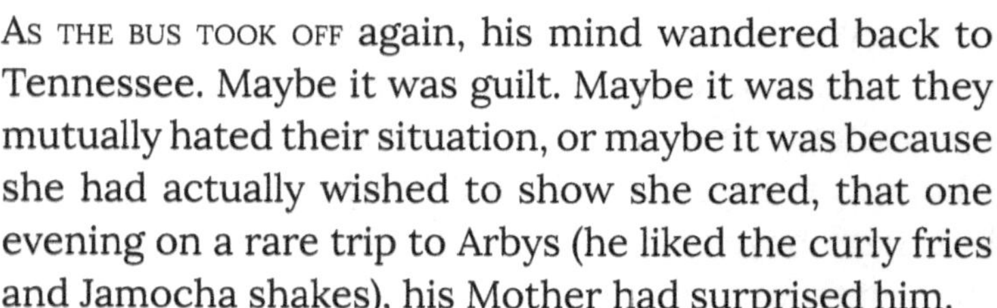

AS THE BUS TOOK OFF again, his mind wandered back to Tennessee. Maybe it was guilt. Maybe it was that they mutually hated their situation, or maybe it was because she had actually wished to show she cared, that one evening on a rare trip to Arbys (he liked the curly fries and Jamocha shakes), his Mother had surprised him.

"Scott" she said, "I know how hard you have tried to help me here. Honestly, it's been tougher than I thought."

So? He wished to scream it, but he remained silent.

Addison continued, "I know you miss your grand-parents, Honeybunch..."

"Mother! Not here!" Scott said.

"...And your drums. And now that we've settled in..." She paused and handed him a large paper bag marked with *The Music Shop* logo. "...I had a little money and..." She teared up. "...I want you to be happy, so, here."

He took the bag and looked inside. The first thing he saw was an Evans practice drum pad. It made it a lot easier, more professional, than using his desk or the wall. He took it out and smiled. "It's not even my birthday."

Addison said, "It's the best I can do right now, but it works well and it's not so noisy."

Oh! Now I get it! He kept silent.

The second thing in the bag was a pair of drum-sticks: Zildjian. His smile brightened. These were the real deal! Then he rolled them over. He saw his Grandfather Stanley's handwriting wood-burned neatly into the upper end of each stick: S.S.S.S. Now it was time for Scott to tear up.

"I asked your grandfather to sign them for you," said Addison.

Scott didn't know what to say. There, on two pointy sticks of blond and beautiful maple, was an acknowledgment of his existence, not just by his grandfather but also by his mother. *Shocker!* He slid his chair back, raised his lanky frame and went around the table to hug his mother, something he had not even thought about doing for a long time.

Addison stood wearily to accept the hug. "So, that's all it takes to make you happy, a couple of pieces of wood?"

"It's not about the wood, Mother," he said, but he would not say more. He still wondered if she had given the gifts because she felt bad for moving him or as payment for his giving in, again, to her wishes. It didn't enter his mind that the giving was because she might love him.

THE SQUEAL OF BUS BRAKES and a nudge from Rubiks Boy brought him back to Colorado. "It's my stop," said the boy, who needed to get out of the seat.

Scott looked around. The bus was stopped on

Gallapego Street, a long way away from Acoma. He had missed his stop. "I'll get off with you," he said. He gathered his backpack and moved toward the front. *Figures!* Even though he had ridden the bus, he would still have to walk. The perfect end to a perfect day!

9 | To the Heart

SCOTT SCHYLER WALKED THE six blocks from the bus stop to his apartment in silence. The only rhythms beating in his brain were the failures of the day; the biggest being the struggle to communicate with a girl. She seemed nicer on the bus and willing to overlook some of his earlier peccadilloes, but his quick reaction to her having his stick was rude, and he had no idea how to recover from that. *Sure, "greatness comes by your attitude!" Ha!*

As he climbed the stairs to the apartment, he hoped to avoid his mother, but that was not to be. He heard the apartment door slam, and Addison met him on the way down. "Come on, we have to go!" she said.

Startled, Scott asked, "What? Can't I put my stuff away?"

"Your grandfather is in the hospital. We will eat on the way." She dashed onward. Again, he was forced to keep up.

Now what? Scott yelled at her, "Can you give me a little clue?"

"What do you want to know?" she barked right back. She stopped and clicked the key fob to unlock the car door. "Get in! You know your grandfather. You are over there enough." She got in, slammed the car door, turned the key, barely waited for him to wedge himself into the little car, and moved off into traffic with hardly a glance. She kept talking. "He's fat; he doesn't eat right; he's got sleep apnea, and his heart flutters."

"How can you be so cruel?"

She shot back, "It's just the truth. Your father had the same problems, and he would not do anything about it. We are left to deal with the mess—"

"The mess? What about love and honor and 'til death—"

"It was not supposed to happen so soon! You think you are the only one who lost someone? You think you are the only one who feels all alone? My parents have been gone a long time. You never even knew them. And you spend more time with your grandparents than you do with me!"

Well, yeah, with that attitude! Scott clammed up. He didn't want to cut his mother any slack, but her honesty was refreshing.

They rode in silence past McDonald's, KFC, and anywhere with food. She had forgotten food and he could understand that. As each mile passed, he was becoming more worried. *Now Grandpa? Is there something I can do?*

THE FIRST THING SCOTT saw were tubes. Tubes hung from a plastic bag and were stuck in Grandpa's arm. Tubes were strapped to Grandpa's nose. Oh, and wires. Wires were attached to Grandpa's chest, and there was also a wire that was clamped to Grandpa's finger. All seemed to be connected to a large machine that beeped at regular intervals. *Was that a good thing, or bad?*

As he finally got past the mechanical horror of it all, he realized his grandfather was asleep. His breathing seemed terribly slow and labored, but at least he was still breathing. Scott wondered how close to death he really was. He had never had to see it this close up. It was also starting to sink in that, with both his dad and his Grandpa's health, he had sort of known there was a problem, but he had not really given it any thought. *What could I have done anyway?*

His grandmother looked up to see him and his mother at the door. She went to Addison first. "Thank you for coming." The women hugged, which was not unusual, but Scott often thought it superficial. This time it seemed different, and rightfully so.

"You know we have to be here," said Addison. Scott was not sure she spoke with sincerity or with obligation. *Curious how we all play such a game of caring.* Then: *Wow, you can be as cruel as your mother!*

Scott's mother asked, "How's he doing?"

Grandma Ray didn't answer her. She turned to Scott and grabbed him as if she would never let go. Here there were no cookies, no chocolate milk, just a little old lady who needed someone to show her they cared. Scott hugged her hard and long, attempting to give her back some of the warmth she had given him over the years.

Grandma looked at Scott and his mother through

tears. "I about lost him," she said. "He was working in the garage and his heart gave way: that damned arrhythmia thing again. I found him on the floor holding his chest. How was I supposed to move him?"

She stopped, broke down again, and recovered. "Anyway, I called nine-one-one and here we are."

"Is he going to die?" Scott blurted.

Addison gasped. "Scott, don't be so rude!"

He thought he had sounded rude too, but how else do you ask?

"They're going to keep him for a couple of days and watch his heart. He'll probably need a pacemaker, but they are worried about his size most of all. Don't get fat, Scott!" She attempted to jest, but she spoke truth. "Speaking of fat, did you guys eat yet? I'm starving."

Scott said, "You guys go. I want to stay here." He walked to the side of the bed and looked at Grandpa's large hands, now wired for sound and medicine and whatever...

"We'll bring you something back," said Addison.

Scott sat beside the bed. He wished to hold Grandpa's massive, kind hands, the same ones that had carved Moses and had carved S.S.S.S. for Slim Scott Stanley Schyler. They had worked with their hands, side by side, but had never really touched. *Why not?* He reached for the rough, strong fingers of a carpenter/woodworker/artist/thinker. *How do you get to be this?* He closed his eyes, listening to the measured beep, beep, beep of the machine, unsure of what all was happening. He grew curious about all the equipment and hoped the sounds were productive.

Silent questions poured out of him like unhappy rim-shots, each one stronger, more intense than the question before: *First Dad, and now Grandpa? Why me? Why any of us? What did I do to deserve this? What did I do?*

Grandpa's left hand squeezed as if in answer. The big man rolled toward Scott, and he opened his eyes. He didn't remove his hand from Scott's. When he tried to speak through his oxygen mask, his voice was ragged and tired. "Hi, young man."

"Hi, Grandpa."

"What's new with you?"

"Nothing. We came right over."

"There's a lot better places to be." Grandpa Stanley started to laugh, but he wheezed and took a deep breath instead, fogging up his oxygen mask. Scott didn't know what to say, so Grandpa continued, "How was your first day back at school?"

Where should he start? Now did not seem the time to talk about all of his Steve Martin, Mr. Ogre, and red-haired girl woes. "It was alright," he said.

That was never enough for Grandpa. "So, what one thing did you learn?" Stanley Senior didn't much care for school drama. You were there to learn, and he was much aligned with Scott's mother; it was always better to be "smarter than the average bear." He asked, "What can you take with you from your classes?"

"Grandpa, now's not the time—"

"Sure, it is. Tomorrow, I may be here or not."

"Don't say that!" Scott shot back.

"But it's true. What you learn will stay with you. What you learn will help you deal with..." He breathed slowly and attempted to breathe deeply. "...with shit like this. What grabbed you today?"

Scott pondered the question, then spoke, "I want to be great, Grandpa."

"Great? You are great," his grandfather replied. "Where's this coming from?"

"Not like that, Grandpa. You always think I'm great, but every time I try something, I get yelled at or laughed at, or I get treated like I'm not even there. This guy says that your attitude helps you be great, but I think it's a bunch of bull."

"Well, there's different kinds of great," Scott's grandpa offered. "People nowadays think we should all be superheroes. That's not reality. There's lots of great without being noticed."

Scott immediately thought about the difference between Dr. Seuss' Whos, and the Amandas, Bethanys, and Steve Martins of the world, and even the girl on the bus, Cheri, who seemed like she was trying to help. Was it because she cared, or because she just wished to be *somebody*? Is that the way it was with his mother? *What about me?*

"I get noticed Grandpa, but it all comes out bad. I hate my life, and my school, and how I don't know how to talk to people, and how I stumble..." He thought of the band room and the bassoon.

Grandpa Stanley tried to sit up. He was very weak,

and he motioned for Scott to help him. Scott maneuvered all the wires and tubes, and he readjusted his grandfather's pillow, after which, Grandpa emphatically reached again for Scott's hand. He breathed deeply and began again. "So, what you just said, isn't that all your attitude? I bet people see you a lot differently than you see you."

"Yeah, but…" Scott stalled, looking for a way to rationalize his thoughts.

"No 'yeah buts'," Grandpa scolded. "I'm in a hospital bed and not sure when I'll get out. I can whine, or I can make the best of it. Sounds like for you, it's a lot of whine."

Scott turned red and pulled his hand away from his Grandfather's. "So, what do you want me to do?"

"It's not about me, it's about you," he answered. "What do you want to do? Start with what you know. What are you good at?"

"Not you too! My teacher asked me that… Nothing… Well," he went on after actually thinking about it, "I play the drums pretty good, but no one's seen me enough to know that."

"They will."

"When?" Scott asked skeptically.

"They will. What else?"

"You taught me to carve pretty well."

"It's not about me!" Grandpa's voice, though weak, was rising in intensity. "Your attitude, your wish to learn, is the point here." Stanley removed the oxygen mask. "Pretty well," he hmphed. "Pretty well? That pterodactyl you carved was nearly perfect. It might even win a contest." His voice was fading faster into fatigue.

"But there are things I should have done…"

Grandpa Stanley forced air into his lungs so he could make a point. "It's not always you. It was partly the wood you chose; that is a learning thing. It was partly experience, which is also about using what you have learned. It is partly about knowing you can do, and not stopping at the first sign of messing things up! Boy, you can be hard on yourself!" He folded back into the bed. "What if?" he whispered.

Scott had to ask him to repeat it.

"What if? Instead of saying, 'I can't,' you say, 'what if?'" He took Scott's hand again. "I've never been *great*; I haven't conquered the world. I have 'masterpieces' that'll never sell. "But I have asked myself What if? a lot." The breathing machine kept time as it blew oxygen into the room. Stanley the Elder put the mask to his face and took a gulp.

Scott waited to hear more from one of the few voices he knew he could trust.

"Great I am not," said Stanley, "but I have asked: What if I tried to really love a woman? What if I tried every day to appreciate how she loves me and my mess? What if I just try my best every day without putting myself down? It seems to have worked. I don't know everything—"

"You sure seem to, Grandpa—"

"Thanks, but do you know why?"

"Why?"

"I started to change how I looked at my world. I wondered: What if I learn instead of complain? What if I listen to others and try what they say? Do I want to be angry all the time, or do I want to be at peace with who I am?"

"Are you?"

"I think I could go today, Slim Scott, and be a happy man."

Scott reacted in horror, "Don't, Grandpa!"

"When the time comes," Grandpa replied. "This is tough stuff for a young man like you, but it really is all in your attitude."

"Where have I heard that before?" Scott smiled despite himself. "It takes people a long time to learn some things doesn't it, Grandpa?"

"It's what you do with what you have. Listen to your heart and not what other people think. Most of the time, they'll never even know or care." Stanley Senior settled back to the bed, drained and tired. "End of sermon! You do what you need to do... And carve me something grand!"

"Like what, Grandpa?"

"Think of what you genuinely care about, then show that care through its design. It's got to come alive. Whatever it is, give it freedom!"

Stanley Senior coughed, then smiled. He finally let go of Scott's hand so he could strap his oxygen mask back on his head. The sixty-three-year-old bear of a man, who just so happened to carve squirrels, otters, and eagles, and who loved to teach others how to succeed, rolled over to get some sleep.

"Thank you, Grandpa," Scott whispered. He wiped tears with part of the hospital blanket. For a long while, accompanied by the beeping of the machines, he was alone but not really. It was a different alone, and it was quiet. He sat and thought about *What if?* until his mother and grandma returned with cheeseburgers, and strawberry Jello for Grandpa Stanley.

Scott's stomach rumbled, and so did his brain. *What should I carve? What do I care about? Who do I really wish to be?* He thought his brain hurt as bad as his grandfather's heart, then decided that must not be true, but it got him to thinking.

10 | WHAT IF?

THE DRIVE HOME WAS much quieter than the one to the hospital. The future was a big unknown and battering Scott and his mother like an Eastern Colorado tornado. *What if?* thought Scott. *Is it really as simple as thinking that it could be positive?*

"Is Grandpa dying, Mom?" Scott asked. He needed to be closer, less formal. He wanted his mom and not a mother.

"We all die..."

Scott gaped at her in disbelief. She sensed his anger and removed some of the edge from her voice, "Sorry, Scott." It sounded like she meant it. "It's been a rough day. Are you okay?"

Why should I be? That would have been his usual blurt. Instead, he tried something new and asked, "Are *you* okay?" This would set off a lecture on all that was not okay in his mother's life, *but change my attitude, right?*

Addison looked at her son as they pulled up to a light. "No, Scott, I'm not."

Scott waited. To hear her be honest like that, and not be defensive, was odd.

"We've moved around so much, and I've tried to figure out how to survive, with you too, and I get so confused, and I change my mind, and sometimes... I'm not sure why I'm even on this planet."

They both sat in silence. *Such a rare thing...* Usually, they were yelling, or they were as far away from each other as they could get.

Addison stepped on the gas as the light changed. "Why am I telling you all this? You don't deserve this burden."

Now he was not sure he should answer. Was she sincere, or just looking for notice? Was it just another round of "I'm here"? "You always say I'm your burden, Mom. You always say I'm bad, or in the way, or dumb."

"Oh, Honeybunch, that's not true."

"Yes, it is! Since Brocco-Roni!" *And a zillion times since!*

"Scott... Scott, I don't mean those things."

"But they hurt, Mother! I'm in high school. I'll be driving soon. Haven't I shown you I can be trusted? You tell me I'm smarter than... You want me to be smarter than... You want me to be professional. Every day I try not to piss you off! All I get is treated like—"

"Oh, Honeybunch—"

"Mother, I'm not three!"

"But that's who you are to me. You may be Slim to your dad, but to me, you're sweet and thoughtful, and smart—"

"You never tell me I am! You always tell me I should be!"

An uncomfortable silence fogged the Hyundai again. They reached the drive where she stopped the car, but she did not rush out as usual. They both looked past each other to the griminess of the parking lot.

Scott spoke first. "Mom, why do you hate my drums?"

"Why, I don't hate them—"

"You don't let me practice; you don't want to hear me play. You tell me I'm worthless—"

Addison evaded, "Scott. I love you so much. *Maybe.* I want you to be happy. *Really?* I know I don't always slow down to pay attention." *For sure!*

Scott was at a loss. *What can I believe?*

Addison sat, awkward and itching to flee. Hostility crept back into her voice. "You know what?" his mother asked, "I want us both to be happy! But there are things that happen. There are some days I think you should live with your grandparents because I do not know how we are going to make it another day. I rarely get the feeling you wish to be around me. I don't think you give a rat's ass!"

"Mom!" Scott gasped. That was as close to cursing as she got. It sounded oddly honest.

"Oh, do not sound so shocked. You think I am mean to you. You think I do not love you, but deep in my heart I want what is best for you. I want you to be prepared for anything. You are amazingly smart, and it frightens me. I wanted music when I was a girl and my choices..."

Scott looked at his mother. He felt he was finally hearing a human being and not some battery-powered robot voice. He kept listening, in hopes that it was all real.

"More than anything, Scott, I... I am afraid. You want

me to tell you the truth? I am afraid. Absolutely, I am afraid of losing my Little Bear." Addison blinked and rubbed her eyes as if there was something in them. What he saw was a want-to-be powerful woman opening herself up to her son.

"Grandma calls me Little Bear," Scott said. He was not sure he had ever heard his mom use the phrase.

"Yeah, and she's right. Except the little part. You are *my* bear, and I struggle to make sure you are fed and clothed. I lost your dad; I cannot even think what I would do if I lost you. It hurts even to see you off to school."

"But I'm fourteen, Mother!"

"That's what scares me. Soon you will be off somewhere, playing drums or whittling—"

"Don't make fun of me!"

"Oh, Honeybunch. Scott, I am not. I am jealous of you and your smarts and your passions... and your chance to talk to a friend like your grandpa. He is so good to you... What if we both lose him? How will *we* keep us?" She broke down in tears and swiveled away from him in embarrassment. "Damn your hearts! What is it with you guys and your hearts?"

Now, she performed her exit-the-car dash, leaving Scott sitting alone. *Well, that was fun while it lasted...* He watched her strut away, but he was shocked when she stopped mid-stride and turned around. She came to his side of the car. He opened the door, but he remained seated as she had him trapped inside.

"Scott, please hear me. I love you. I love how you are

so dedicated to learning the drums. I love how dedicated you are to whittling. I love what a strong, professional, young man you already are, and so eager to learn." She reached inside the car and offered Scott her hand.

He didn't accept her offer.

"I know you may not believe this, but I want you to know that, even through my mistakes and my fears, I want you to become who you wish to be. I maybe have never said this before—"

"You haven't!" Scott would not cave so easily.

"Well..." Addison was put off, but she rebounded, "... Maybe I can show you better."

"How?"

"Well... change takes time. We'll have to help each other."

"How?"

"Well... First, I guess we need to stop asking how and come up with a plan." She said, attempting humor.

"Ha ha, Mother," said Scott. "And stop saying, 'well.' You know better!"

"I... I was trying to have some fun—"

Scott spoke angrily, "I don't want your fun, Mother. I want you to hear me. Sometimes I think I'm not even in the room. I have ideas too, Mom, and hopes and plans, and sometimes I need your help too!"

"So, what if I say I will try to work better with you from now on? What if we could start teamworking a bit?"

"No promises, Mother! Like Grandpa says, unless you can follow through."

Addison answered, "I promise I'll try to follow through. Does that work?"

"So, what do we do to start?" asked Scott.

"You tell me."

"Can we really talk to each other and be honest? I feel like we're sort of doing that now."

Addison would not wait any longer. She reached for Scott and pulled him, with some force, from the car. He was not prepared for that and looked at her in fright. She placed one hand on each of his shoulders, and she looked him square in the eyes. "Slim Scott Schyler, this seems to have been a good step in the right direction. Do you feel a little better?"

Scott nodded, and he did not struggle under her authority. He asked, "What if we try this again?"

"When?"

"Whenever it starts to get crazy. Can we just slow down, or ask each other to slow down, so we can think things through?"

Addison looked at her son. "I'm going to have to change my attitude."

"Grandpa and I just talked about that," said Scott.

Addison became defensive again. "About me?"

"No, Mom. About... about everybody. Grandpa says it's the only way to work with others, by working through yourself." He let out a sigh. It had been a hellacious day; he wondered if he would ever see his pillow.

Addison asked, "Will you walk with me to the door?"

He grabbed his backpack from the backseat while she waited. *She waited!* They did not hold hands; that would have been weird, but they did match step, in rhythm, up the stairs for the first time in maybe ever.

THIRTY MINUTES LATER, Scott had found his second wind. He bounded down those same stairs, this time with his mother's permission! *What if I just ask?*

After a quick call to the hospital and the discovery that Grandpa was awake again and doing well, and after discussing with his mother a project he needed to start on, Scott grabbed his bike and headed for the house on Cherokee. Grandma wanted him to check that all was safe; he wanted to work in the shop. "Just keep your fingers," his grandma had said on the phone.

"Yes, Grandma," he grinned at the same old joke.

Addison had relented, with maximum hesitation. "I guess you can go. Just be safe. And only a couple of hours; you have school tomorrow." Then, she had walked down the dreary hall of their apartment and closed the door to her bedroom. No goodbye, no hug. *Oh, well...*

As he worked his bike out of the apartment garage, Scott pounded himself with questions: *What if I try to be more friendly? What if Mom begins to hear me?* Then: *Naw, don't push it!*

He answered himself, "Attitude—*all is attitude.*"

Shut up! he retorted.

The conversation changed as he pedaled closer to

the shop. *What if I can do this? What if it truly becomes something?* He remembered what his grandfather said about carving and most things in life. It was a cliche, but he was learning: anything can be done if you take one step at a time.

It was these steps he was contemplating as he carefully crossed Bannock, pulled up at the Cherokee house, placed his bike along the wall, clambered up the stairs, touched Moses, turned the key, and entered a very dark, incredibly quiet, house. There were no cookie smells, no Grandma hugs, no sawing, scraping, or sanding sounds from the garage; there was only silence.

He flicked on the front room light, moved to the kitchen, and thought it only fair that, as he was doing a service—inspecting the house—he should have a glass of chocolate milk. Gathering what he needed: milk, spoon, glass, and syrup, he created his favorite concoction.

Taking a swig, he sought out his grandpa's laptop. He could have done this step at home, but it was better here. He had some research to do. Strange how that sounded different when it was for something that mattered, rather than what you had to do at school.

He downed the last drop of milk, rinsed out the glass, and put all the items back where they belonged. Grabbing the laptop, he went behind the house to the garage and opened the door. Here was Grandpa. The place oozed the aromas of pine and cedar and the glory of life. Things were created here that had meaning.

"Make me something grand," Grandpa had said.

Scott spoke out loud to an empty garage, "I'll do my best, Grandpa."

As he switched on the lights, it was gloriously bright, and he could swear he heard Grandpa tell him, "I know you will."

Slim Scott set the laptop down on the work bench and started step one. He went looking in the storage shelves and found a large slab of cherry wood and a piece of spalted maple. He really liked the lines in the wood that looked like veins. They would look great in what he was planning.

He measured each piece carefully, planning to first create two-inch by two-inch blocks of each wood type, then glue them together to create a cube eight by eight inches. This would give him plenty of room to carve. He measured and marked, three times, then pushed the big red ON switch on the table saw.

He stopped, feeling the silence even more as the powerful blade spun. *I'm on my own. Do not f--- it up!* He would not say the word in his grandfather's garage.

A few minutes later he wiggled his remaining ten fingers, and he announced to the room, "Good job." The sound echoed as if his Grandfather had said it. He found glue and clamps and spent the next hour creating his block.

As the block dried, he got to work on the research. What do I care about? What do I wish to see come to life from inside the wood? He Googled, he took notes and sketched. He would not begin carving until he was ready, as Grandpa had continued to show him. The cool thing, he decided, was that he would have plenty of time to work on this during Thanksgiving break.

When he finally thought about stopping, the clock over the bench read one o'clock. *I have school tomorrow! No, today!*

He yawned and poked his pterodactyl. It cast odd soaring shadows as it swung in the light. He decided he had better call his Mom to let her know he was on the way home. He checked and cleaned his workspace, grabbed his notes and the laptop, then took one final look around. "Listen to your heart," his grandfather had said.

"I'm working on it," Scott said aloud. He smiled in satisfaction as he shut off the lights.

11 \ Smyrnaean Blood

S COTT WOULD HAVE LOVED to stay in the shop all night and the next day and the next, but that was not to be, even if it was the last day before Thanksgiving break. School was important to his mother and to his entire family. Honestly, it was important to him, the learning at least, if not the people.

As he leapt the two steps off the bus and onto the sidewalk, Scott was hoping, like every other student in the place, and like many teachers that had to be there because they could not find a sub, that it would be a day filled with movie watching, texting, and friendly chatter. He knew that might not happen. Lately, teachers were required to keep on keeping on, even if the students were zoned out.

His first class of the day, the one he had completely missed yesterday because of his mother, was, Scott knew, not going to go well. Trying *What if?* here probably would not make a difference. Scott's not so private hell was gym class. It was not the actual exercise: the running and the jumping; although he knew he was scrawny and clumsy, he always tried to do his best. The hell came more from the public performance. There were jocks and then there was Scott.

He shuffled into the locker room in dread and heard the same kind of comments he had heard yesterday on the bus: "Who are you? You supposed to be here?" These were the harmless and obvious questions. Then it got worse. As he was searching for an out-of-the-way locker, where he could change from street clothes to gym clothes, and where he could avoid as many eyes as possible amidst the incessant clank of slamming locker doors, there came a voice he recognized.

"Hey, Honeybunch! Guys, it's Honeybunch. He's back for round two!"

Scott watched Steve Martin force his way toward him through the students who were getting ready for class. "Mommy let you come back today, did she?" Steve Martin now had an audience and he puffed up like a rooster at a cock fight. He swooped in on Scott, talons extended, as if Scott were a sickly animal. "Your mommy's not here today, Slim." He slithered. "What are you going to do now?" He backed Scott into the lockers and stretched his neck to get in Scott's face. His stance was iron hatred.

Steve Martin was more dangerous today. He was in an arena, and a bully must live up to expectations. Student murmuring rose as boys gathered to watch. Scott knew some kids felt exactly how he felt because it had happened to them. He also knew they were grateful that the searchlight had moved on to another soul. Why did everyone always rely on someone else to deal with a Steve Martin? Of course, Scott didn't want that job either.

Scott's head began to pound; he opened and closed his hands into tight fists. He remained silent, but he turned all sorts of cedar-toned red. The honeybunch inside him felt about three, and he wished for his dad to help, certainly never his mother.

Outwardly, he prepared for battle; his rooster's chest expanded as he breathed deeply, and he tried to grow even taller. He held his ground, but he remembered his mantra: speak only when necessary.

"Don't you talk, Honeybunch?" goaded Steve Martin."

The crowd grew around the two, some beginning the chant: "Fight, fight, fight."

Steve Martin's fists raised, locked and loaded, ready to throw a punch. Instead, he body-slammed Scott, toppling the tall one into the lockers. Gasps came from every direction. Scott lost his wind and he doubled over to breathe.

Steve Martin backed away, looking at Scott and his cronies and classmates in snide victory. Some students chuckled, but mostly there was silence as they wondered what would come.

Scott stood tall again and gulped air. He did not move at all, but he wanted to. He had been here before...

IT HAD HAPPENED IN SMYRNA. It had happened because he was angry—angry with his mother for moving them, angry with his dad for dying which had forced them to move, angry with his grandparents who would not stop the journey, angry with himself for... *For what?* Somehow it had to have been his fault.

Scott had never been a fighter. He was constantly reminded by his mother: Blessed are the peacemakers. *But what if they don't want to make peace with you?*

His first day at Thomas High, the second school he had moved to in Smyrna (due to his mother's job), was illuminating. He had already discovered that people in the south speak slower. He liked this because he often felt people spoke too fast; he liked to take in the words. He also was learning that there were other colors of people in the world. In Englewood, at least in his school anyway, while there were a few Hispanics, it was mostly Whites. In Smyrna, there was a much more even mix: Black, White, Latino, Asian—due to the job opportunities.

Truth be told, he had never really considered color. He had usually considered niceness and politeness: his mother's expectations. If you were nice to him, he would be nice back. It seemed to work well that first day too, for a while. But this day's illumination was that no matter where you went, there were always people who wished to show their power over you. Some Smyrnaeans were no different.

At lunch, he had entered the cafeteria to the sound of clattering plastic trays and dropped silverware. The smells of institutional food hung in the air as a hundred twenty or so students gathered their tater-tots and pizza, and the soggy vegetables which no one ever ate.

Scott sat down at one of the long, too-low-for-his-legs cafeteria tables, expecting to eat alone. He was taken aback when a petite girl, wearing a bright yellow blouse, joined him. He was reminded of Amanda at *L'Orange*. She sat right next to him and she smiled!

Why? He said a curious, "Hi?"

She grinned as if the ice cream truck had just pulled up and said, "Hi" back. Then she started talking like a greyhound chasing a rabbit. "I'm Ariel. I was named after the girl in *The Little Mermaid*. Do you like math too?"

Scott realized she had been in his algebra class. He nodded.

"It's so boring," she said, "I've got it mostly figured out already!"

"Me too," said Scott.

"Can I have a tater-tot?" she asked.

He shoved the tray her way.

"When's your birthday?" she asked. "Mine's in August."

"Hey, mine too." They seemed to have a lot in common, except that she talked a lot. What was it that had brought her to his table? *Why would she want to talk to me?*

She answered his unspoken question. "It's fun to meet new people. Everyone here knows everyone else already."

Scott took a closer look. She was so bright and pretty and... Oh yeah, she was Black, with extraordinary blue-black hair. It was as shiny as her attitude! Scott found himself enjoying his lunch, and he began to relax, happy someone had noticed him.

Unfortunately, Ariel was not the only one observing. Apparently, he was sitting at the wrong bench. From across the cafeteria, he heard a boy yell to the person sitting next to him. "Hey, Joey, you see the new kid?"

As Scott looked up, the nameless questioner was immediately answered by Joey. "Yeah, it looks like he's at the wrong table." Two boys stood and weaved their ways through the benches. As they neared, Ariel seemed to shrink.

Scott scanned the room. Two teachers were near the milk station flirting, a third was grading papers. None of them had heard, or had wished to hear, the possibility of trouble. He also noted that he, a tall, white boy, was one of only a couple of people who had breached the color barrier. Scott had learned about the rules against segregation in Social Studies; here the students had not gotten the message.

The two boys, Joey, who was stocky and snarling, with a crease in his forehead—Scott thought maybe a horse had kicked him? —and his, so far nameless, side-kick who was also stocky but taller, strode to his table and squeezed in. Joey sat to Ariel's left and the other boy next to Scott on his right. There was nowhere to run. There was barely room to move his arms.

Joey said, "Ariel, you know you shouldn't be here." He could have been scolding a puppy, but his face was nowhere near as cute.

Ariel turned off her sunshine. "It's my cafeteria too!" she said.

"But not this table!" answered Joey. He grabbed her paper carton of chocolate milk and poured it onto her tray, splashing and soaking her yellow blouse. Ariel's assertiveness waned. She remembered where she was and who she was. She dropped her head to her chest.

"Dusty," Joey continued, "where should Ariel be?"

Scott connected the name. It was the color of Dusty's hair, the dirty browns of his clothes, the name more friendly than he appeared. *He should be called Shit.*

Dusty had played this game before. "Outside eating the lawn."

The two Smyrnaeans laughed.

Under the table, Scott pumped his fists open and closed like a heartbeat. *Blessed are the peacemakers!* This show was mostly for Scott's benefit, but he was pissed at who they were picking on.

Joey glared at Scott. "You don't want to be sitting next to this cow do you, Slim?"

Here we go... Scott was not sure which he was most upset about, the *cow* remark or the *Slim.* Either way, it was not going well. He wiggled to stand, but his legs were wedged. It would take sizable effort to move, and Ariel might get hurt in the process. He pulled one hand at a time out from under the table and began to strike it enough to rattle the plastic trays. Students at nearby tables looked up from their meals. Scott did not speak.

"Are you a stupid cow too, Slim?" Joey asked. He saw Scott's fists; he heard the pounding, but because there was a body between them—Ariel was hunkered down in a protective ball—Joey did not register any danger. "You look like it, sitting next to this—"

Joey didn't voice his next word; he couldn't. Scott had been discovering a friend in a wonderfully ebullient young lady, and he wished to protect her. He reached his long, left arm over Ariel and in one, swift, smooth, strong motion, he placed his hand behind Joey's head and slammed it into the cafeteria table. Ariel screamed as she ducked, trapped between two dangerous beasts. Milk and tots went flying, as did two of Joey's teeth. Dusty only stared while Joey struggled to stand up, but Scott kept him pinned to the table, then he grabbed a handful of hair and tugged his head upward to slam him back down.

Dusty screamed, "Mrs. Alberson, the new kid's picking on Joey!" The teachers had heard the slam, as had most of the school, and charged to the scene.

"Dusty, get some napkins," said Mrs. Alberson in the classic—I'm in charge here now—teacher voice. Blood was dripping from Joey's mouth and nose.

Still stunned, Dusty asked, "Wha—?"

"Napkins. Now!" Mrs. Alberson looked at Scott and demanded, "Take your hands off him."

Scott's hand remained in Joey's hair, wrapped like one of Moses' talons around Joey's head. He spoke clearly and intensely. "He called her a cow."

Mrs. Alberson didn't hesitate. She grabbed Scott by his hair, pulled him straight out of the cafeteria bench and onto the floor before he could blink. She kept pulling until the teacher who had been grading stopped her.

Scott looked up from the floor, still angry and not ready to give in.

Ariel got up crying, her yellow blouse now speckled in dark red, Smyrnaean blood. She ran sobbing to the girl's restroom. No one followed.

Joey sobbed too, smearing blood around his face with the napkins. Dusty ran outside to the slide. Student diners erupted into chatter, but they were soon calmed by the teachers who sent them outside, and who should have been paying better attention.

Then it was standard operations. The principal had called Mother to school and said, "I don't think your son is a good fit... Two teeth and a broken nose... Joey's parents won't press charges if..."

Mother is livid and screams on the way home, "How could you do this to me?"

Within the week, Mother had thrown in the bloody towel and they had headed back to Englewood.

BLESSED ARE THE PEACEMAKERS. If Scott was going to ask—*What if?*—it might as well be here. He rested against a bent, gym locker drawing deep, angry breaths. Steve Martin had turned his back. It would be so easy to... *Am I supposed to just sneak away?*

But what if I do not draw blood? He didn't want a fight; he wanted peace. He held his ground and, as calmly as he could, he asked so all could hear, "What did I do to you?"

Steve Martin wheeled, and his talons came back out. "You exist, Honeybunch. You just are. You ought to just spin your ugly little self right down the toilet, so I don't have to look at you!"

Scott grinned. Somehow, his brain connected to his algebra class and the logic problems they had been learning. Steve Martin had not answered the question. Scott took a step toward the bully. Maybe it was something in Scott's eyes; Steve Martin took a small step back.

Scott repeated, "Yes, but what did I do to you? Are you just mad that my mother hugged me goodbye? Does your mother not hug you?" Scott was not sure it was worth it to try to reason with this rooster, but wasn't it better than ending up in the principal's office? He kept his hands to his side, but he did brace his legs for a further attack. Around him students sniggered; but this time, Scott saw they were on his side.

Wishing to show his world—"I'm here!—Steve Martin had not expected anything but retreat. Now he was trapped and defensive. "My mother hugs me."

Scott smiled, loving the set-up. "Good," he said, "because you sure could use one." He reached his open arms in grand gesture toward Steve Martin like Grandma Ray would do for him.

For slow seconds no one stirred. Finally, a couple of people caught Scott's wisdom and they laughed, and that laughter spread from kid to kid. Steve Martin, now red-faced and alone, stomped from the room.

Scott's fear dissipated. He was prepared for more trouble, but he did not expect it. He found an empty locker and sat down on the bench. Students went back to their business; the show was over.

As he finally began dressing out for gym, in the classic colors of Euclid High: washed out gray, which was supposed to be silver, and black, he felt rather pleased with how he had dealt with this incident. It was certainly different than in the past. He had avoided a fight, and a fight on his second day at a new school was not the way he wished to be noticed.

He had felt bad about Joey, still did. He felt for Steve Martin too. Why did people have to be so cruel? What caused a person's vision to be so cloudy? So hateful?

He pulled off a Frankenshoe to replace it with a gym shoe. He pondered those two boys. *Obviously, I am not the only one with problems with my anger.* While this didn't make him feel better, what he had just done in holding that temper was a good start. He smiled.

Then he remembered where he was. *Oh no, gym class.*

12 | SPECTACLES

As the boy's locker room at Euclid High School emptied, Scott stood to exit as well, but he had one more decision to make. His glasses were a daily gym dilemma and a superbly ironic Catch-22. He hated them, but clearly (*ha!*), he had to wear them to see. While not blind, his nearsightedness was definitely a factor in his athleticism. However, to wear them was to invite potential breakage and the wrath of Mother for wasting good money.

So, what would it be today—blindness and peer derision or the possibility of parental punishment? Since one option was the same as the other, Scott tucked his glasses inside his Frankenshoes, blinked a couple of times, closed the locker, and shuffled to the gym.

Here, his ears were accosted by the tennis shoe screeches and the rhythmic thump of basketballs on solid, polished maple. Students dribbled, passed, and shot a dozen basketballs, and they yelled—mostly yelled.

Scott might have enjoyed playing basketball, if not for other students. He knew the rules; he had aced previous written tests. Since there were no courts at the apartments, he practiced baskets at Grandpa's. It was calmer there, more private. He often found the basket! *Maybe 'cause you can see! Duh...*

Scott walked, now a blur among blurs, across the gym floor to introduce himself to the teacher. He was looking for familiar, friendly faces, faces he might have overlooked during the stand-off with Steve Martin. Where had he gone? Even a blind man could hear his rant, but it was absent. The beat of the balls to the floor echoed throughout the large, dim room. Lights were lowered to save energy, making it even tougher for Scott to see.

As he walked, he saw students peering at and behind him. Not unusual. But, as he followed their gaze, a basketball rocketed into the side of his head. Stunned, he staggered but did not fall. His right ear stung deep red and was ringing. His classmates began the assault of laughter to his senses, again, and his emotional heart throbbed as painfully as did his physical head.

"Steve Martin!" The booming voice did not match the little round and balding man that Scott vaguely saw coming toward him. Once an athlete, the sidelines and home-brews had given him a look of a gnome, but power remained in his voice. He growled at the bully. "Sit down. Do not move!"

Steve Martin smirked as he took a seat in the bleachers. "Yes, Coach. Sorry, Coach," he kowtowed."

"You're sorry, alright. You want to play today? Shut your mouth." The coach turned to Scott, still swaying from the ball blast, and touched him on the shoulder. "You alright?"

Scott nodded.

"I'm sorry about that introduction. I'll deal with

that later. I'm Coach Danforth," He held out his hand. "You are?"

"Scott Schyler." He accepted Coach's hand.

"Well, welcome, Scott. Go have a seat. Take a breath. Let me know if you need anything."

Scott nodded and sat in the bleachers far from Steve Martin.

He looked at Coach Danforth and wondered if there would be consequences, but he was not sure it mattered. The coach wore a whistle and, progressively, held an iPad and not a clipboard. Even though it was November, the coach wore baggy shorts and a Euclid sweatshirt. It was amazing what you could get away with if you were a gym teacher.

Danforth called the class to line up at specified spots along the edge of the basketball court. Scott was happy to sit, but he found himself in the fishbowl again as all eyes faced him. Steve Martin smiled smugly at him from his right. Scott winced, then shrugged. *You're in the bleachers too, bonehead!*

Coach Danforth took attendance on the I-pad, calling names while his class became antsy. Someone dribbled a ball and the thud echoed throughout. "Hold the ball!" yelled Coach.

It was class tournament day, conveniently the day before break. Coach could sit, watch, and grade with little investment. He had them choose teams. "Greg James, Mark Adams, The Eric, Steve Martin, you're up. Remember, everyone plays!" *Even Steve Martin? How do teachers forget so easily?*

Groans abounded from students at Coach's admonition. Scott was not the only one apprehensive about playing. In gym class, it was hard-core athletes versus the schmucks. He knew he was a schmuck.

Two more things he knew: One: he would be the last one chosen. And two: he would most likely sit on the bench all game. He shrugged at this thought. If called on to play, he would run, guard, and try his best, but all the while he knew he would never be trusted enough by anyone to feel the ball in his hands. *What would I do with it if I got it?*

Coach turned to him. "You okay to play?"

Scott nodded.

"Good, we'll get you settled in. We're all friends here." *Right!*

Scott looked at the team captains and did some match-up math. Four teams—five players each—twenty students. Steve Martin is the last captain; I am last called… *Oh crap!* The only other person he knew was Eric, from band. Why was he in freshman gym? Why had Coach called him *The Eric*?

Teammates were chosen first, then friends, then "that kid." There were cheers or boos for each in turn, and each name called pushed Scott farther into his zone defense. His head bowed in full ostrich mode. *I'm not here. I'm not here.*

"Slim." Steve Martin glumly called on the boy in the bleachers. Neither was happy at this turn of events.

"Not gonna happen!" bellowed Coach. He pointed to Scott. "Eric, take this one. Mario, switch to Steve's team."

Mario, a boy Scott didn't know, but who looked like he could use fewer donuts and more laps around the gym—*Be nice!* —shuffled to Steve Martin with disappointment. Scott breathed a sigh of relief and rubbed his temple. But was this better? The Eric looked like a jock; he acted like a jock. Would he intimidate like a jock? *Only one way to find out.* Scott stood and timidly made his way toward his newest new team.

As if in answer, Steve Martin piped up, "Have fun, Honeybunch!'"

The Eric sneered. Coach Danforth's voice boomed again. "Can it, Martin!"

The Eric looked at Scott. "I see you've already met Steve."

Scott shrugged.

"Are you any good?" Eric asked.

Scott shrugged again. He would try his best to listen, to see, and to not suck.

Whistles blew. Pounding was the ball, and pounding was Scott's head as he kept pace with his team up and down court. He could do little harm if he never got the ball, so he committed to being involved, for whatever it might be worth, and he even attempted to get open. He really would not mind, for once, excelling... Well, at least doing okay and perhaps being a part of something. *What if?*

As the game continued, The Eric acknowledged him some, a silent urging-on that broke through the thuds of ball and hoots of crowd. Scott wished to perform, and in an instant, quick as the toot of a whistle-blown foul, his chance popped before him. A nameless team-mate, obviously not knowing any better, took a tremendous chance and passed him the ball.

Scott caught the thing—some miracle—and stood flustered. This was not supposed to happen. He dribbled a couple of seconds and stopped. He pushed up his glasses that he realized were not there.

Now, what to do? He pivoted and dribbled in place. His heart beat in rhythmic pressure, pressure, pressure. The sports cliches piled on: time slows, ball drops into basket, crowd roars at victory. Scott had sense to realize he was too far from the basket; he would have to pass. He wished only to once step out of himself, to see beyond who he was. He scanned the floor for an open man.

From the sidelines, there were many shouts. One stood out. "Pass it for your mommy, Honeybunch!"

Man, that guy! Steve Martin was right though. His mother would expect the best; Scott would attempt to step up. With the rhythm of nervous inferiority thudding in his ears, he found a possible receiver. He pivoted, dribbled, and passed the ball. The gym went crazy!

But not in a good way. A whistle blew. Strangely, it was held by some nameless blob that also held the ball. In his terror of opportunity, he had thrown the ball to the student-referee. Steve Martin's howls, and a host more, thrust into his chest like hot lasers, melting every last atom of dignity.

You'd be laughing too, if you were them... What God allows you to be so stupid?

Because all of life does not come down to just one

moment, the ball was put back into play. The Eric did not look at him, which was alright. With his face red, he retreated to the sideline. He had been benched.

Thankfully, however, not everyone is a Steve Martin. As the game continued, Scott saw that his team was losing, with or without him—some sort of consolation. The Eric called, "Time!" Scott stayed far out on the fringe of the huddle.

The Eric was appropriately, coachingly indignant. "You guys are not listening to each other! You're running around. No, not really. You're not really running. There's no hustle. Do you guys even care?"

Halfhearted nods showed the depth of concern. This was not the Final Four; this was ninth grade gym class; this was barely for a grade. And it was the day before a nine-day vacation.

"Give us a break, Eric," said a nameless teammate. "This is gym class, not State! Just 'cause you're going doesn't mean we are!"

Ah, thought so. He is a jock. Scott felt even worse.

The Eric ignored the voice. "C'mon, guys, we can do better than this. I mean, hell," he looked at Scott who squinted back, "what's your name?"

"Slim." An unknown answered for him.

"Yeah, Slim. Even he's got more hustle. Man, he was trying at least. He might have screwed up, but at least he was trying; he was moving!" Scott's eyes opened wide at the recognition. *Well, that's something!*

"Now, let's do this. Slim, you're in for Alex; watch who you're throwing to!" said The Eric.

The team broke. The whistle blew. Scott never touched the ball again that game, but something was different. True, he had not made the big play. He had been hooted off the court because of a mistake. But it was more. It was the fact that a jock, The Eric, had said he was... What? Mediocre? Attempting to attempt? But it was positive.

Games were won and lost. Eric's team (*My team!*) had won; Steve Martin's had lost. In fact, Steve Martin had never made it onto the court, having been benched by Coach. He was still pouting in the bleachers. *Thank God for small favors!*

Scott wondered how people learn to react the way they do. What was the difference between The Eric and Steve Martin?

As he opened his gym locker he sighed with relief. He reached for his glasses, cleaned them on his shirt, and placed them gingerly on his sore head. At least this once, in someone's eyes, he had been noticed for something good. More, he noticed a positive in himself. He had not struck back when he could have, even when others might have expected it and even approved. Because of that, he had played and helped his team, while another was left on the bench. *What if? Indeed.*

13 | Parradiddles

PERHAPS IT WAS LAST night's talk with his mother. Perhaps it was how he had held his tongue— and fists—against Steve Martin. Perhaps it was a small boost from a high school senior everyone called The Eric. Whatever it was, Scott's confidence was riding higher as he moved from class to class. In English, he ventured a smile at Sarah as he sat down. He even went so far as to say "Hi." She acknowledged him with a nod as she placed her books under the desk, which he did not kick.

Miss Walters wished them all a good Thanksgiving, then gave them an assignment for over break. The students' reactions were typical: "Groan, Complain, Groan."

"Please write, in one hundred words or less, about viewing greatness in your lives," she said. She cautioned, "Greatness is not always about winning the big game. What kind of greatness do you see around you? What greatness do you see in others?"

Since it was the day before break, she said they could use the rest of class to get started. Most kids got out their phones and texted to someone across the building or, in some cases, across the room.

Scott put his head into the work. It is what he had been taught to do, plus, no one wanted to talk to him anyway. Maybe he could finish the thing and have less homework over break.

Rodney edged to his desk and asked, "What will you write about?"

Scott reverted to cranky, "Why do you care?"

"Whoa!" said Rodney. "You're a tough crowd!"

Scott looked at the other boy... *What if?* He would try small steps. "I don't know yet," he said. "You?"

Rodney replied, "Maybe my parents. Naw, they're boring. I know. Maybe The Eric."

Scott replied, "What's he to you? Why does everybody call him that?"

"He's awesome!"

Scott had never heard anybody talk about a fellow student the way Rodney was gushing all over this kid. He asked, "What, are you his brother or his boyfriend?"

"What? Huh? Gee, no, it's not like that..." He thought best how to explain. "You know how a lot of students are wannabes? Best at this, best at that, but it's all for show?"

"I've met one already," replied Scott. He rubbed his ear, reliving gym class.

"Oh yeah? Who?" asked Rodney. He was eager for gossip, and it was a way to get closer to Scott.

"Steve Martin."

Rodney asked, "How'd you meet him?"

"You don't know? It was all over Facebook." Scott explained his introduction to school, then gym class. "What grade is he?"

Rodney laughed wickedly. "He's a super-senior. Too

cool for school, so he keeps flunking. He might be here forever. Don't feel bad, he picks on his own mother."

"Don't we all?" asked Scott.

"No one's a fan of Steve, not even his friends. Naw, The Eric is no Steve Martin. Steve is a wannabe. Football captain? No way. Best grades? Steve can't spell A, B, C, but he can spell F! Best attitude?"

"I've seen that!" said Scott.

Rodney added, "The Eric's gonna be valadict—"

Scott completed the word, "Valedictorian. So, why's he in ninth-grade gym?"

"He is? He must have missed some credits," replied Rodney. "Hmm. I guess we all learn. The Eric is the man, man. He even talks to freshmen."

"So, what's he doing in a bad band?"

"He's Ogre's T.A. Eric says he's getting ready for college. He's got a music scholarship already at UNC."

Scott broke in, "What's he play?"

"Everything. That's why he's The Eric. Sports, grades, girls too. Everything!" Rodney grinned. "I hate him."

"Yeah, me too," said Scott. He glanced at Sarah who had moved across the room to sit with Darla. He paused. "He didn't seem like a jerk in gym. He sort of stuck up for me; I mean, who does that?"

"Yeah, that's why I hate him. He's actually a good guy. Nobody should be that nice. I think that's why I'll write about him."

The two boys chatted until people began to fidget before the bell. Miss Walters chimed in with, "Have a happy Thanksgiving!" Some students even answered.

She moved to Scott. "So, how's your second day?" she asked.

"Pretty good," Scott lied.

"Scott, I'm really curious about your writing. You spoke so well yesterday, I'm anxious to see what you'll have to say."

"Okay," he said. That was lame, but he didn't have a better answer. "Have a good break, Miss Walters."

"You too, Scott." She turned to Rodney. "You too, Rodney!"

Rodney waved, leaned into Scott, and said, "Wow, second day and you're already teacher's pet." He sang, "Te ee each er's pe eh et." He took off for band like a shot as Scott glared at him and started to chase him.

Scott saw Sarah and slowed down. Did he slow because he wanted to act more grown up? Or was it because he just wanted to watch her? Yes!

Day two of band began differently. As the boys arrived, The Eric saw Scott and waved to him. "You're right," Scott said to Rodney before they broke for their places. He parroted what the trombonist had said earlier, "Nobody's that nice."

Scott climbed the risers to the drum section where he was surprised to see Anthony; it was the last day and all. Anthony nodded and pointed to Scott's position. There, on the music stand, was a brand-new folder. *Well, how about that!* Scott said, "Thanks." He opened the folder and skimmed the music.

The main band room door slammed; students jumped

as the bell had not even rung yet. Mr. Ogden strode to the front of the room in no mood for pre-Thanksgiving-break fun. He motioned for Eric to move away from the podium, and he took the senior's place. Timid protests issued from various areas of the band.

Mr. Ogden ignored these and started right in, not waiting for people to get set up. "Sarah!" he boomed. "Concert 'A' please."

Most people were still talking and randomly tooting; even Sarah was still wetting her oboe reed. She nervously finished adjusting her mouthpiece. Mr. Ogden's voice climbed again above the ruckus, "Sarah, Concert 'A'... Please!"

Sarah blew one solitary note and held it. She breathed, blew, and held it, and breathed and blew again until, finally, the band was nearly a unit. Scott stood politely at attention, unsure of his part. He had not found warm-ups in the folder, so he mimicked Anthony's strokes quietly attempting to learn. Looking even farther left, he saw The Eric, also keeping time.

With a stern, double circular, arm motion, Mr. Ogden cut the band to silence. "Today's my turn," he said. "You guys were pitiful yesterday, pitiful! I know none of you practiced overnight. We'll see. We'll see today... It's pop-quiz time on *Frosted Fanfare March*."

Groans abounded.

"Get it out, now. In silence. Can you do that? Get it out now!"

Off to Scott's far left, in the horns, someone knocked over a music stand. No *pressure here!* Scott looked for the chosen music, found it and placed it on top of the others. He began to read it while he pantomimed the sticking.

"Drummers, we shall start with you. You had two missing members yesterday. Hope they learned something in their banishment." He looked at Anthony and Scott in disdain. "We'll start at measure forty-six to the coda. Forty-six to the coda... We'll do it as a group. If it sounds like crap, we'll listen individually."

Mr. Ogden raised his arms impatiently, allowing milliseconds for each drummer to get his or her act together, and began the count: "One, two, three, four; one, two, three..." His right arm found the beat and dropped on four, and the drummers took off—in about seven different directions. Some had not found measure forty-six; one kid was still finding his music. It seemed Eric and Anthony had done well; they continued to play until Ogden cut them all off.

"Great! Just great..." Mr. Ogden drew out the word in a sarcastic, Tony-the-Tiger-like growl. "Dumb-Dumb drummers. We'll take it one at a time then. He looked at his grade sheet, saw the new name he had penciled in, and he announced, "Mr. Shooler! Schooler?"

"It's Schyler, sir." *Polite, speak when spoken to, but what if I add a touch of courage?*

"I don't give a crap if it's Sylvester the Cat."

So much for that! Scott slipped a couple of notches backward on the attitude scale.

Mr. Ogden continued, "Did you look over the music like I asked you to do yesterday? Did you look at it at all?"

Mr. Ogden's double speak grated at Scott's brain as he pondered the question. There was no way to tell the Anthony story. It would all sound like an excuse and cause needless trouble for Anthony. He wanted to lie, but that was not who he was either. "No, sir," he replied. This should open the door to be able to explain.

Mr. Ogden had assumed his own truth. "Well then..." He smirked. "Well then, we'll do what we call a sight-reading test. Do you have the music?"

"Yes..." He forced it, "...sir."

The band director snarled in return. "Can you... Can you play?"

Scott's ball-thumped ear was pounding; his eyes locked on the band director. "Yes... Yes, sir." *Why do I always have to find the Steve Martin's of the world?*

"How long have you been playing? How long?"

Scott answered simply, "All my life."

The class snickered. *At least that was in unison.*

"Silence!" Mr. Ogden's eyes clouded with anger. "Mr. Shooler," The director drew the word out like a native Tennessean. "Mr. Shooler, here at Euclid, I make the rules. I want straight answers to straight questions. So, Mr. Shooler, I'll repeat the question. How long have you played the drums?"

Scott's expression didn't change but his voiced turned to ice, "And I'll repeat the answer. All my life. And it's SHY-ler."

You could have heard a piccolo drop.

Mr. Ogden breathed deeply, in control, but his bald head glowed in sunset reds, betraying how he really felt. He wanted the day to be done. He wanted to be done with this student. "We'll see… We'll see." He angrily turned the pages of the three-ring music binder. The pages should have caught fire. "If you would find *Prospero*, by Angelica Brown."

Scott started to look for it as The Eric broke in, "But Mr. Ogden, the band hasn't even looked at that yet!"

"That's why they call it sight reading, Mr. Sanchez. You'll learn that… You'll learn that in college."

The Eric could do nothing more than watch.

Scott had found the music and was going through the arrangement.

"I'll give you the correct beat," said Ogden. "Start at the top and you're on your own, Slim."

Damn him! thought Scott.

Rodney watched the tall new kid turn crimson. Sarah saw too. Her reaction was to clutch her oboe tighter to her chest.

"This is cut time, Slim, one two, one two. Watch me to come in." Ogre counted and clapped: "One two, one two; one two, ready play."

Scott played.

Miss Walters had asked him what he did well. Here was the answer. His grandfather asked him to think, "*What if?*" Here was that opportunity. Anthony had seen this boy play without sticks. Today he got to see the real thing.

From first single stroke to ghost notes and rata-macues, Slim Scott Schyler played. He did not play to announce, "I'm here." He played because the beat was in him; it *was* him. For Scott, the rhythmic sounds of one simple snare drum playing the fourth snare part of a mediocre march was a triumph in freedom.

Scott played from the first to the last measure through the coda. Although he had never seen the music in his life, his timing was impeccable. Each note was proper volume, length, and style. Scott's technique was proficient and professional. But it became more. Technique turned to creativity and while he did not go off score, he embellished, he enlivened the music. More than simple, tap-tappa-tap, tap-tappa-tap, the beat sang through his mind, it flowed through his heart. It was the pulse in his head against all his life, transported through his arms, his wrists. And his groove inspired others.

His audience was hypnotized. Scott continued to play, buried inside the music. So buried, he didn't, for a time, hear another drum pick up near him. The Eric had joined in, playing a second part, intermingling the rhythms to form a stronger sound. It was unexpected. It was a pre-Thanksgiving treat. It became something to say you had been there to hear.

As all eyes were on them, the senior and the new kid played as if they had played together forever. They looked at each other for cues, twists and turns. The drummers reached the end of the score, and then they took off on their own. They could not hide their enjoyment; smiles gleamed from ear to ear. Finally, they nodded to a conclusion. The concert closed to silence.

Scott, now panting and in a sweat, folded his drumsticks together and sat down. He humbly bowed to Eric as he did so, and the gesture was returned. He was feeling, for once, victorious.

Students, for as long as their attention spans would allow, remained rapt. A deep spent breath from the lone oboist down front broke the silence. Anthony leaned toward Scott and whispered, "Wow!"

Mr. Ogden had wanted to make a lesson of this young, rude, awkward beast of a boy. He was perturbed and ready to throw an eraser. By the end, however, his attitude had changed. He had become as engrossed as the students. As Sarah took her breath, so did the teacher take his. Student heads turned as Mr. Ogden's hands came together in appreciation, one man applauding another for work well done. The room broke into full applause.

As had to happen, the mood was broken. Although appreciative, Mr. Ogden would offer no more to Scott than what he had given. He continued to test each drummer and then moved to the Brass Asses. Eventually, the bell rang. Students began to pack up. A "Bwa-bwa" came from the Rodney trombone.

Sarah smiled at Scott and asked, "See you on the bus?"

Scott dipped his head toward her in acknowledgement. Inside his heart was aflutter.

The Eric and he met on the way out the door. "Happy Thanksgiving, Scott."

"Thank you," answered Scott.

The Eric turned away and Scott stopped him. "No... I mean, thank you for gym class."

"And thank you for just now; that was a blast!"

The rest of the day was a blur. People who had seen him in band acknowledged him in the lunchroom. They did not sit with him, but some nodded or smiled. His other classes were mostly people-on-their-phone sessions. He sat and watched others, air drumming and reliving a—*maybe-not-so-small?* —success. He also thought a lot about what Rodney had said about The Eric. *How does one become The Eric? What if?* He would have to start with becoming a Scott first.

14 \ Tastee-Freeze

SO, LOGIC WOULD TELL us that A + B = C, thought Scott, as he climbed aboard the bus. If A is: "Scott is riding this bus," and B is: "Sarah is riding this bus," then C must be that they live close by. *Algebraic logic problems in real life!* Then: *God, you are a school kid.*

So? What if I ask her?

What if she says no?

Scott climbed the steps, nodded to the driver, and walked to where he had sat yesterday. He looked down to see the acne-prone Rubik's player already in the seat, spinning the colored squares with vigor. Instead of sneering (like a Steve Martin might do to him), he tried a "Hi," then went even further, "Can I sit with you?"

The boy looked up. He didn't speak, but he did move his backpack.

Scott asked, "What's your name?"

"Matthew," said the boy, his braces glimmering in the afternoon sun.

So, where do I go next?

Matthew picked up the conversation, if you could call it that. He held out his well-used and very dirty cube. "Do you wanna try?"

Because Matthew's other hand held a Snickers bar, and because half of that bar was now coating the cube,

Scott declined. "No thanks, Matthew," he said, "but thanks for the offer. Do you ever win at that thing?" Scott asked.

"Oh sure," Matthew replied, "I just pull the pieces off and put them in the right places."

Scott grinned and thought that was likely. "Uh-huh," he said.

Sarah was not on the bus yet, so he wondered where she might be. Even thinking of her had his heart doing that flutter/beat thing.

Out the window, Scott spied her across the sidewalk in the parking lot. His flutter turned to thud. She stood next to Darla and was talking to... *Damn it!* Of course, it had to be The Eric. *Why him?* He could not tell what they were saying, but it seemed way too playful. He punched the back of Sarah's seat.

Then, as Scott watched, Sarah hauled right off and pushed Super-Student as hard as she could. The Eric, surprisingly, stumbled. He almost fell, but he caught himself and then, shockingly, he reached for Sarah and gave her a big hug. It sure looked like she accepted it too. Scott punched the seat again. Matthew said, "Hey!" The bus driver looked up from her coffee.

Scott's heart pounded. He scowled and tried to breath. *Geez, you barely know her. Chill!*

He continued to watch as the trio broke up. The Eric walked away with Darla. *What the heck?* Sarah, now all smiles, weaved through students and onto the bus.

What do I do now? He had been gearing up to talk to her all day. It had been a decent, somewhat positive day, but apparently it had been too much of a good thing. He poked his glasses up his nose in disgust.

Sarah reached her seat, saw his sulk, and asked, "What gives?"

Scott hesitated, he took a breath... and stalled again. Then he dove in. "What was up with you and The Eric?"

"He made me mad! He wanted to drive Darla home. He wouldn't take me. Sometimes he can be such a jerk."

He tried not to show his elation. "I've heard he has a way with the women."

Sarah scooted her oboe case and backpack across the seat in front of Scott. She looked at the glum drummer and realized what was on his mind. A grin turned to a giggle and then full-blown laughter. She sat down so she would not fall down. "Eric... and me? The Eric? Super cool kid, The Eric and me?" Now she was the one pounding the seat, but it was in uproarious—you have got to be kidding—glee.

Scott turned the color of the emergency lights on the bus. He wished he had stolen Matthew's candy bar and stuffed it in his mouth.

Matthew filled in the blanks. "They're brother and sister."

Scott scowled. "How do you know?"

"I've known them a while."

Sarah confirmed the report. "I baby-sit Matthew and his brothers."

"I don't need to be baby-sat," said Matthew.

Sarah and Scott took another look at Matthew's

chocolate mess, and they broke into laughter. Sarah reached into her backpack and handed him a Kleenex. "You were saying, Matthew?" Then she confirmed the information. "Yes, Eric and I are brothers.

"But Vaughn and Sanchez?"

"What are you, stalking me?" It was Sarah's turn to blush. "You do pay attention, don't you? He's my step-brother."

"Oh… You sure shoved him hard."

"He deserved it! He thinks he's all that. And he sort of is. I try to keep up with him in music, but it's tough. He's really good. Well, you saw. So were you."

"So, Darla and he?" Scott was trying to verify that he could flutter again.

"They've dated a few times."

Where do I go from here?

Scott and Sarah both tried to speak at the same time:

He: "I'm sorry for yesterday."

She: "That *was* pretty cool today."

"Oh, sorry, you go…"

"No, sorry you go…"

They were Jack and Jill, both in that tumble of words falling down politeness hill.

A chocolate covered mess spoke. "Why don't you both go?"

"Shut up, Matthew!" Sarah and Scott spoke together, and all three laughed.

The bus driver closed the door, shifted, and a bus load of students set off toward Thanksgiving break.

Other sounds in the bus seemed quiet, far off. School breaks were difficult for many; having to deal with being at home was sometimes worse than going to school.

It's now or never. Keep going Scott! What if?

Sarah started up again. "The thing you did with the drums today... Where'd you learn that?"

Scott hesitated, not wanting to brag. That was a no-no with his mother. *But, you know what? I did good.* "Like I told Mr. Ogden, I have played a lot. I learned on my own."

"Yeah, even Ogre was impressed. And then Eric kicked in with you. It was like you'd both done that forever!"

"Yeah, that was pretty neat. I wish everyone was like that."

"Me too," said Sarah. "He's my brother, but he's pretty nice."

Scott pushed up his glasses that didn't really need to be adjusted. He tried to think through the next step. "Um... What are you doing next week?"

"Nothing."

There was stark, uncomfortable silence for too long. *Come on Scott!* He breathed deeply and forced out the question, "Do you want to do something?"

"Like what?" Sarah's facial expression gave nothing away as to how she really felt about the possibility.

"Well, we must live close. Do you ride bikes?"

"Only one at a time."

"Ha ha. But that was quick!" They laughed. Scott's flutter grew from moth's wing to Moses' whoosh.

"We could..." He stumbled and then picked it up, "... we could meet at Tasty-Freeze and ride around." As he waited for her answer, he felt like Moses was crash landing.

"When?" she asked.

Now would be a good time to die! How could you ever have a better day than this one?

THE DAY BEFORE THANKSGIVING turned out to be mild, mid-sixties and sunny. But, in terms of the food, it was a chili sort of day. Chili dogs and chili cheese fries from Tastee-Freeze were the main course.

Sarah and Scott sat across from each other. She was snarfing down more fries than even Scott could shovel in. They had spent a good portion of the morning biking around Englewood. He had explained the street alphabetization. *Nerd!* But she had stayed interested. They had crossed Bannock three times and survived, and they were tired and a little... *Wait for it!* ...chilly. They were warming up both physically and to each other.

Scott was feeling comfortable, as evidenced by a neatly polished wooden Triceratops setting between them near their drinks. He had been afraid she might laugh. She had not.

"You never did answer me," Sarah said.

"About what?"

"About the S.S.S.S. on your drumsticks. I can understand three initials, for Scott, whatever your middle name is and Schyler, but the fourth?"

"You'll think it's silly—"

"No more than a wooden Triceratops." She smiled.

"Okay." He was taking lots of chances. "It's because of my dad. Don't laugh. He and my grandpa both call me Slim."

"But you hate that!" said Sarah.

"Not from them. After Dad died, Grandpa gave me a drum set, Grandma too. In fact, she's the one that got me started. Dad always called me Slim, 'cause I am. Grandpa calls me that, because he wants to be slim.

"So the four esses?"

"Easy. Slim Scott Stanley Schyler."

"Aha!" Sarah paused. "Sorry about your dad," she said.

"Yeah," he said.

They parried over the last of the fries while Scott thought of another What if?

"Hey, we're not far. Do you want to go see the shop and meet my grandparents?"

"Well, I sort of have to get home," Sara said warily.

Scott kept up the sales pitch; he was excited to show her off. "We can have chocolate milk and maybe cookies for dessert. Grandma's a great cook. And you can meet Moses!"

"Who's Moses? Does she already know we're coming?"

Scott answered both, "You'll see." Then, "Doesn't

matter. She's always got stuff, er, food out. Grandpa says it's why he's so fat!"

Sarah reached for her phone, texted her parents, then disconnected. "We'll have to go quick."

Scott could have flown. Instead, they hopped on their bikes.

Three blocks later they pulled into the drive, stacked their bikes, and climbed the steps. "Here's Moses," said Scott.

"Wow, this is awesome. Hi, Moses. Your grandfather is talented. I see where you get it."

"But so are you; you play three instruments."

"Six, actually: piano, guitar and flute too. I've got to keep up with The Eric."

Scott opened the door. "I'll start calling you The Sarah!" *How can anyone smile this much?*

That answer met them inside. "Grandma, this is Sarah," said Scott.

"Pleased to meet you," said Grandma Ray, reaching for both of them. She bound them in the world's greatest hug. The youngsters turned reddish again at how close they were, but Grandma's eyes twinkled as she toyed with them. She let go and reached for a platter, then asked, "Chocolate Chip or Oatmeal Raisin?"

"Grandma, we just ate," said Scott. He attempted polite refusal even as he wished to chow down.

"I didn't make 'em for myself. Your Grandpa doesn't get any..." She turned from frivolity to concern.

"How is he, Grandma?"

"He's actually asleep... Sarah, I would love for you to

meet him, but... We were at the doctor's again today. They gave us more medication. The doctors are still having trouble with the atrial fibrillation." Both youngsters gave her a quizzical look. She responded. "His heart is beating too fast."

She put down the cookie tray and reached for the un-cookied hand of each child. She squeezed both for a long time. Sarah didn't seem to mind. "Pray for him. Eat a cookie in his honor." She let go of their hands.

"Or three," said Scott. "Chocolate milk too?"

"Oh, Scott, I'm out of Hershey's," answered Grandma Ray.

It was not from selfishness that Scott was disappointed. That just never happened. All was not right in the world.

"Did you come to show Sarah your next project?" Grandma asked.

"There's more? I've already seen the Triceratops. Now Moses. What next?"

Grandma Ray re-grabbed Sarah's hand. "He's being really sneaky about it. He won't even tell his own grandmother! Go! Both of you."

Scott had wanted Sarah to meet Grandpa Stanley. It was weird to know he was nearby but unavailable. With cookies and no milk, they walked out back to the garage. Scott opened the door, turned on the lights, and shivered. The room was cold and lonely. Everything remained untouched; Grandpa had not been out there for a while.

On the bench was a checkerboard-like wood block,

sort of on over-sized Rubik's cube. There were pencil markings on it, but it had yet to be carved.

"So, what's the big secret?" Sarah asked. She wrapped her arms against herself to ward off the chill.

"My dad was always sick," Scott began. He could not remember when last he had talked this much to one person, and now he was going to try to describe a dream that was only a seed of an idea. *Here goes...*

"What Mother thought was laziness, and what I thought was not caring, was Dad's heart not pumping. He'd work all day, then come home and sleep on the couch. I thought he hated us. His heart just couldn't keep up, and no one knew."

"Same with your grandfather?"

Scott dreaded that answer. "It seems like it."

"So, you're making your grandmother a heart? Cool, like Valentine's Day." She wanted to have fun with him, but he shut her down.

"No... No..." Scott sighed. *How do I explain this?* "No... A model of a real heart. Here, look at this." He picked up his drawing and a picture of a real human heart.

Sarah gave him a peculiar look. "Sorry, Scott, that's ugly. It's like a piece of meat!"

"No, it's beautiful. It's an amazing piece of equipment. It's almost its own musical instrument. Look." He showed her the diagram. "Blood enters here, in the vena cava; it moves to the right atrium, goes through these valves, like sliding glass doors, I guess, and then it gets pushed into the lungs..." His chatter was non-stop at his discoveries.

Sarah grasped his enthusiasm; but was not sure she wanted a biology lesson. She smiled politely and tried to listen.

"...Then the blood picks up oxygen, comes back into the heart and goes through two more pipes, the aorta and the descending aorta, to get oxygen to the whole body."

"Um..." Sarah was at a loss to even know what to ask.

"But it's so cool." He saw her interest fading, and he wanted her to feel his eagerness. "This lump of meat moves all of our blood all through all of our bodies faster than once a minute—forever. Forever." He repeated the word in his own fascination. "If it's not perfectly in rhythm—every time—you die. Forever." He was nearly out of breath.

Sarah asked, "So, how does it know how to do that?"

Scott thought... "Electrical impulses, I think. I know they had to shock Grandpa to get his heart pumping right again."

"So, where does the heart get the electricity?" Sarah asked, trying to see how this all worked.

Scott was stumped. "Umm... Is the heart like a battery?" He thought of how his phone had to be recharged. "I don't know," he said. He grabbed his notes and wrote down her question. "I'll have to look that up. Thanks, Sarah."

"Glad I could help," she joked. "You're really into this. So, what's wrong with your grandpa?"

"It seems like a few things, but it all comes from

the heart. Grandma called it 'cardio-myopathy,' some disease that's inherited, that's why Dad got it—"

"And maybe you too?" Sarah was beginning to understand Scott's deeper interest.

"Yeah, maybe me too."

"So, what's cardio—mya. What's it do?"

"Everything. No blood, er, no oxygen in the blood..." He had been trying to see how this all worked, and it helped him to speak it. "...The kidneys can shut down and you die. Or the lungs shut down and you get congestive heart failure... and you die. If blood doesn't pump correctly through your legs, you can get a clot... and you die. Or, if you get a clot in your brain, that's a stroke—"

"Yeah, I get it! Holy cow, Scott, That's a lot of death!"

Scott grew quiet. He felt the conversation was wearing on his new friend. He finished the lecture. "There's just so much we take for granted. It's why Grandpa can't breathe. It's why he's so big... It's a nasty circle: no oxygen equals no energy; no exercise equals fat; too much fat equals no exercise which equals no oxygen. Without a good beating heart... How are you supposed to win?"

Sarah didn't want to be rude or sound stupid, she just wasn't sure what to say. "Your wooden heart won't solve anything—"

"No," replied Scott, "it won't. But maybe I can. I can study, I can read. I get good grades. What if—?"

"You want to be a doctor?"

"I'd never thought about it until now, but—"

"But why an actual wooden heart? Why not just a Valentine heart?"

Scott relayed what he had been considering. "To honor the Schylers: Dad and Grandpa. The word Schyler means scholar. Both of them were, er, are, scholars. I want to make it pretty, and pretty accurate. I'll wood-burn a plaque for it to stand on that says: The Schyuler Heart. Kinda cool, huh? The scholar's heart. Grandpa and Grandma can keep it to remind them of their son."

Sarah looked at Scott in admiration. Scott hoped he had not bored her to tears and scared her away.

He finished his speech. "Grandpa told me to create something grand for him. What is more important than the pulse of life? Maybe when I'm a doctor, I'll put it on my desk."

THE BIKE RIDE TO SARAH'S was quiet. Scott thought about how the first date ever in his life had turned into heart failure, literally and figuratively. *What girl is going to go for a sad scientist wannabe? We should have been laser-tagging or something, not talking about arteries and atria. What was I thinking?*

Scott would have been deeply surprised to know that Sarah was thinking no such thing. Rather, Sarah was thinking more toward a next time. How do you let someone know how special they really are, when they cannot see it for themselves?

The porch light was on at Sarah's. Scott did the

polite thing and walked her from bike to door. Sarah opened it. They stood and looked at each other, both unsure what to do. Scott reached out, took her hand and simply said, "Thank you."

Sarah pulled the hand and long arm toward her. No longer would his Grandmother Ray's be the best hug he had ever received. "Call me, Slim," she said, and she closed the door.

As Scott pedaled up to his apartment, he could not remember how he had even gotten there. Moses could have carried him home. *How can anyone smile this much?*

15 | THE ERIC

SLIM SCOTT SCHYLER WOKE up bright and early Thanksgiving morning; it felt like Christmas. He was wide awake and re-living last night's good-bye. *I wouldn't mind a couple more of those hugs!* He looked at his phone. *Six o'clock... Seriously?* He rolled around for a couple of minutes, then decided that to try to go back to sleep was of no use; he was just too wired. Throwing back the covers, he stretched his long body, got up, and dressed. His mom would still be sleeping, so he would leave her a note and go work on The Schyler Heart. There would be plenty of time before the big meal.

The day was colder, and light snow blew in a brisk wind as he bicycled his familiar path. *Brrr. I should have worn a heavier jacket!*

Traffic was light, and he shivered as he approached Bannock. He slowed, looked both directions, then leaned on the pedals to cross quickly. Somehow, he missed the big, white, FedEx van that rumbled up the hill. Apparently, the driver had not seen him either. The van's brakes squealed.

Scott grabbed his brakes and turned sharply toward the curb. He missed the van, but his front wheel hit a drainage grate, plunged into one of the wide, metal slots, and landed Scott on his butt. His backpack went flying. Fortunately, he had not hit his head. He sat up, looked around, and cussed.

The driver barely slowed down, honked "sorry" and left the fourteen-year-old in a pile.

"Thanks a lot!" cried Scott. He stood slowly and inspected his body parts: a sore rear end and a badly scraped left hand. The bicycle had taken the worst of it. He would have to walk it to Grandma's.

He picked up his backpack and limped forward, pushing his bike. *Is this the way it works? One good thing happens and then fourteen more bad things follow?* There was no perfection, no greatness—it was unattainable. You do the best job you can, and the band teacher gives you a little hand clap but does not talk to you. Most people don't even know your name, much less care about who you really want to be. You get one great day with a girl, and then you get run over by a truck. *What's the point? Can't it ever be easy?* He looked down at his crinkled front tire as it did a roll-thunk-roll-thunk kind of thing. *Obviously not.* He trudged on.

From behind him, a car horn honked. Scott jumped from street to sidewalk wondering if he was going to get hit again. Realizing his neck was sore too, he swung his body around to see a blue, Subaru Outback. It had ski racks on top, and a big dent and a missing headlight on the passenger side. Apparently this driver was in the same league as the FedEx driver.

Scott ignored the car and kept walking. Whoever it was, he was not interested.

He heard the car door open and shut. "Hey, Slim! Scott… Where you going?"

What the hell? If this was Steve Martin, he'd bash the bent bike over his head. He decided it was best just to keep walking.

"Scott, Drummer Boy. Hold up!"

Scott picked up his bike, spun it around and slammed it down, placing it like a barrier between him and whoever was disturbing his Thanksgiving morning. "What?" he pronounced, then he recognized The Eric.

"Are you okay? It looks like you took a tumble," said the Subaru driver.

"From the looks of your car, you coulda done it to me. It's 6:30. What are you doing?"

"It's my dad's car. I had a little mishap with a light pole."

Scott was shocked. "You? The Eric?"

"Don't call me that."

"But everyone does!"

"Well, you're not *everyone*. I'm just Eric" He looked at a broken bicycle and the hand of the broken boy. "What happened?"

"FedEx truck. My Thanksgiving gift."

"Where are you headed?" asked The Eric.

"No," shot back Scott, "where are you headed? It's 6:30."

"I know you can keep time, Drummer Boy," The Eric said. There was no malice. "I work sometimes overnights at the homeless shelter on Broadway."

"Of course you do. Why would I expect anything less

of The Eric?" Scott's tone was not near as respectful.

"Hey, that's not fair."

"How can anybody do all that you do? Be all everybody says you are?"

"*Everybody* doesn't know squat. I just want to be the best at what I do, but I'm just Eric, someone who tries."

Scott remained silent and pondered the older boy's words.

The Eric pointed to the Subaru. "I don't always win. You can ask my dad. No don't. Better not to bring it up again." He chuckled. "You look like you could use a ride."

Scott softened. "Maybe..."

"Are you hurt?"

"I just got hit by a truck. Do you know CPR too?"

"As a matter of fact."

Scott rolled his eyes. "Uh-huh."

The Eric reached for his wallet. "Do you want to see my card?"

"I don't think there'd be any way for you not to be The Eric," Scott proclaimed with a grin.

"Whatever..." Eric opened the passenger side door. "Let me have your bike, and you can sit down. I think you need to. Do you drink coffee?" Eric grabbed the bike. Scott reluctantly let it go. He watched as Eric placed it on the ski racks and found some rope to tie it down. "So, Denny's for coffee?"

"Why?"

"Why what?"

"Why do you want to go have coffee with *me*?"

"Hop in. Let's go get warm." The Eric looked again at Scott's hand. "You're dripping. We should probably get a bandage somewhere. Don't get blood on Dad's car." He grinned.

Scott relented. He sat down, feeling more appreciative than he wanted to admit. His heart was still racing from the accident. *Am I in shock?*

"Thanks," he said, as The Eric closed the door.

Their first stop was to Walgreen's. "Stay here," The Eric demanded, and Scott did. The senior came back out with a small first-aid kit. "Eight bucks," he said, "I hope you're worth it."

"Gee thanks. What no credit card?"

"It's only for college stuff."

"Of course, it is. Why would I not know that The Eric already has college figured out too?"

The Eric slammed the door and looked Scott square in the eye. "Look, I'm trying to be nice to you. You might consider that before I put you back in the gutter."

"Ouch!" said Scott, but he knew The Eric was right. He thought about greatness and attitude. Do the good and bad things eventually even out? *Like an algebra problem:* X+Y=A+B. "Okay, I'm sorry. Denny's it is. I'll buy." *I'll use Mom's emergency card!*

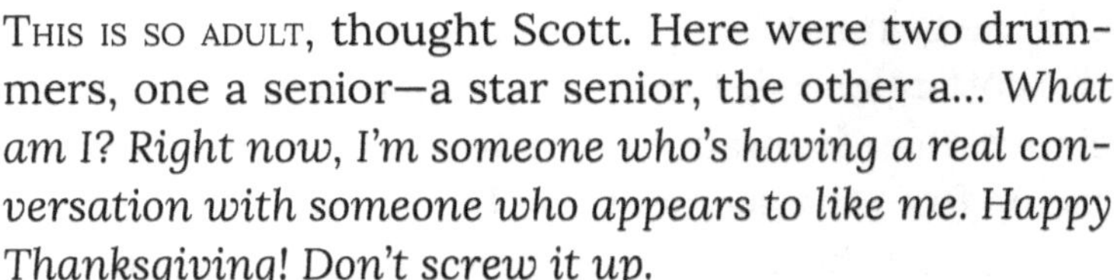

THIS IS SO ADULT, thought Scott. Here were two drummers, one a senior—a star senior, the other a... *What am I? Right now, I'm someone who's having a real conversation with someone who appears to like me. Happy Thanksgiving! Don't screw it up.*

The Eric looked at Scott's beverage of choice. "It's too early for Dr. Pepper," he chided.

"Mom thinks coffee is only for adults." Scott paused, then thought he might add honesty. "Plus, my dad drank Dr. Pepper all the time. I like it better than coffee, anyway."

"Aha! Did he teach you to play drums too?"

"No. I learned by myself. I'm still learning."

"Well, you're ahead of me. I could barely keep up! Your dad must be proud."

"He's dead."

"Sorry."

"It's okay. I'm figuring it out. But what's the deal with you? Band, and sports, and college, and homeless, and stray, little ninth graders. No one is that perfect."

The Eric looked out the Denny's window at the rising winter sun. "What people think I am, and who I want to be, is not the same. I just think it's better to plan for good and not have to fix all the bad all the time." Scott thought of Grandpa Stanley always planning, and he wondered how he was doing.

"Nobody talks this way! No high school kid. How do you know all this?"

"My dad… My step-dad and I talk a lot." The Eric was about to give away his secret. "My real dad is in jail; I think about him, and about what not to do."

Scott sipped his Dr. Pepper, enjoying the warmth and camaraderie as the sun shown. He looked at The Eric with empathy, with the same understanding of loss. "I get it, I guess." Scott's hand dripped again, in heartbeat rhythm, onto the tabletop. The wimpy Band-Aids in the first aid kit were failing. He wrapped his hand in a napkin.

He was trying hard not to be angry at the driver of the FedEx truck, at his Mother who could not make up her mind and forced him into all sorts of situations, at his dad for dying, even at The Eric, who had what he didn't, the ability, the attitude to accept… He was even angry at Sarah for having such a cool brother. "Damn it! "Don't you ever get pissed?"

"Greatness," said The Eric, "comes by your attitude."

"Oh, come on…" Scott spoke in disbelief.

"I had the same English teacher. "I'm helping Sarah memorize… The saying seems to work for me, at least part of the time." The Eric shrugged. "It's late, I need to get home. Where do I need to take you?"

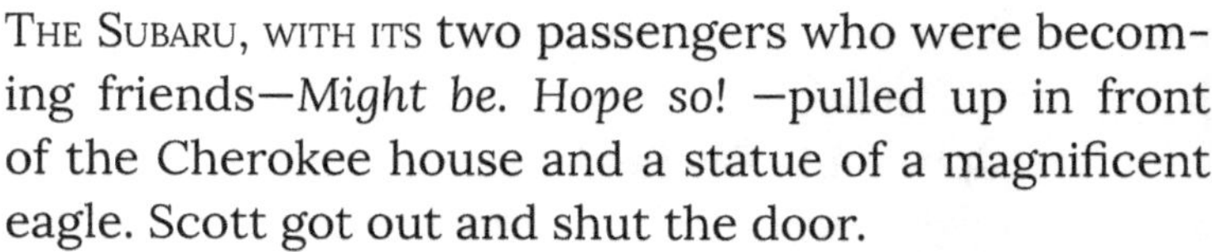

THE SUBARU, WITH ITS two passengers who were becoming friends—*Might be. Hope so!* —pulled up in front of the Cherokee house and a statue of a magnificent eagle. Scott got out and shut the door.

The Eric hit the button to roll down the passenger side window. "One more thing, Scott."

"What?" His brain was on overload, and the information had come from an unexpected source. He needed to process it all.

"The marching band needs a good drum major next year. You'd be good at it."

"No way. Not with Mr. Ogden. How do you stand him?"

"I take a deep breath and know what I want to be."

"Seriously?" *What are you, my grandpa?* Scott breathed in that information, nodded, and closed the door.

The Eric took off like a blue bolt of thunder. *No wonder he hit the pole!* Then, Scott saw the bike, still attached to the top of the car. He yelled at the fading vehicle, but The Eric was already too far away. Scott smiled. Here was a reason to see The Eric, *and his sister*, again!

As Scott stopped to give Moses his ritual pat, he smiled, even though his body hurt. He was experiencing a true Thanksgiving. He tapped on the door; it was too early for him to just barge right in. Grandma Ray met him, looking worn and tired.

"Shh," she whispered. "Good morning to you." Her smile was half-light. "You're here awfully early." She saw the make-shift bandage on his hand and asked, "What happened?"

"I couldn't sleep. A FedEx truck almost hit me. The Eric and I worked on it some," He held up his hand, "but it's still bleeding."

"Come on in, I'll get you fixed up. Anything else broken or bent?" Her whisper was weak and raspy, not like his grandmother at all.

"The Eric. Who's that?" Grandma Ray asked, as they walked together past the kitchen and living room and on through to the bathroom. Scott described his morning, as his grandma got a washrag and soap, and she cleaned his hand.

"How's he doing?" Scott asked. Grandpa was always an early riser. The house was strangely colder and quieter without him up.

Grandma did not answer. Instead, she rummaged through the medicine chest for some antiseptic and began to dab it on a gauze pad to place onto Scott's wound. Her hands were shaking.

"Grandma?"

16 | AGAIN?

GRANDMA RAYLEEN LOOKED AT her grandson. Her heart ached even more than Scott's wounded hand. She put down the medicine and hugged him so tight, he thought she would knock the wind out of him. She began to sob with the weight of forty-some years of memories and love, failures and successes. She reached for a gauze pad to wipe her tears. "I just called your mom," Her voice crackled, "she's on her way over."

Scott stared into nothing. "Grandma?" said Scott, as if asking again would change things.

"He's gone. Your grandpa's heart must have given out last night. At least, as far as I know, he went peacefully."

Now, it was Scott's heart needing to be shocked. He sat down on the toilet and rocked his body as if he were three, his head throbbing along with his hand. His countenance changed in front of his grandmother, and she pulled away from the heat of his anger. He stood, knocking over his grandpa's toiletries on the sink but paying them no mind. He had to get out!

Grandma Ray moved to stop him but thought better of it. Scott barreled past her and past the kitchen— *no cookies and milk this morning*— thought Scott in an abyss of anger and sarcasm.

Grandma followed him. "Scott?" She felt the back door slam, and she whispered, as she had done so many times, "Don't lose a finger."

The lights came on in the garage, but it remained dark in Scott's soul. He yelled from the depths of his pain, "Again?!"

He reached into his backpack and brought out his first ever carving. This dinosaur was his vision of his Grandfather Stanley. Without him, there would have been no Triceratops. Now, he became even more enraged. During the bike crash, the bony frill—the shield around the animal's head—had been torn, and one of the horns had been knocked off. He hurled the beast from him with all his might. It landed under the table saw in a pile of dust, like a forgotten and dejected little puppy.

Without Grandpa... He had lost his heart. Scott bent his body toward the work bench where, methodically and with malice, he struck his head against the maple, rhythmically and repetitively. For how long he did this, he would not remember.

"Scott?" It was a faint, familiar voice he heard, and he began to emerge as from a bad dream. His head was throbbing. *Well duh, Stupid ass.*

"Scott?"

"What?! Leave me alone!" *What could you possibly have to say?*

"I'm sorry for your loss, Scott. I'm sorry for *our* loss, Scott."

"Shut up, Mother!"

"I know you are hurting. Say what you need to say; do what you need to do. I am still here for you."

"Really, Mother? Then why did you let this happen? Twice!" Tears rolled down his cheeks like sawdust to his grandfather's floor.

"Say what you need to say, but deep down you'll find that's not true. I did not do it. You did not do it. You want to blame yourself, but there's nothing you did wrong."

"You could have made them go to the doctor."

His mother, with tears in her eyes too, touched him gently on the cheek. Scott shrank from her touch then relented. She gently took his face into her hands. "Scott, look at me, please."

He glared, but he looked.

"Honey..." She left off the *bunch*. "...Nobody can make anyone really do anything. I have been thinking about this a lot. I am sorry we moved so much; I am sorry about your dad too. I wonder everyday what I could have done different. I do not always get how to fix what is wrong."

Addison let go of her son and wandered the shop. She ducked her head under the swooping pterodactyl, then she placed her hands on an unfinished otter. Scott could not remember her ever having been in here. Looking to the floor, she spied a lowly dinosaur under the table saw. She picked it up and caressed it as if it were her baby boy. "He's still here, you know... They're both still here." She gently placed the Triceratops in front of Scott on the bench.

Scott's face remained wrought with scorn. He had retreated into the silence that had protected him for so long.

"You may not feel that way now, but he is. Just look around you."

He would not speak. *Not now!*

Addison Schyler headed for the door. "We had a deal. When you are ready to talk, I am too. I hate this adult stuff as much as you; I am not always good at sticking things through. But Scott, we have to. We have to. We can. We can do this together."

Her words thrummed through her son. Scott wanted to believe that she was being honest. He wanted to trust, to change his attitude, but this felt like the FedEx truck had hit him again!

She walked away with one last comment. "You don't have to believe me, but I wish you would. I would ask you—what would your Grandpa do?"

"He's not here!" Scott nearly tore the roof off the garage.

"Yes, Scott, he is." She softly closed the door.

A troubled and lonely boy sat quietly for the longest time. No headbanging, no thumping. He just sat. Finally, he spoke to the empty garage and to his Triceratops. "What is this, some kind of test, Grandpa? How many times do you have to get run over?"

Grandpa's first step was to listen. Scott did, but he heard nothing. *What am I listening for?*

"What do you want to see come to life?" These were his Grandpa's words.

He took a deep breath and listened to all that was around him.

There is no one who can answer except you. You must listen to yourself. With your own ears, not Anthony's or Mr. Ogden's. Not your mothers. You must see with your own eyes...

"Damn it!" He swore, not quite ready to believe his own B.S.

He listened anyway. Where might that take him? What if?

The next of Grandpa's steps was to visualize. What did he have to look forward to? What did he have to do?

Scott picked up his carving knife and the Schyler Heart wood block, but he set both back down. In his current state of mind, he would destroy the project—perhaps even create his grandmother's worst nightmare. Already some of his fingers were bleeding and that had not been... *No. It was not my fault!*

Koestenbaum's words drew him. "Greatness comes by recognizing that your potential is limited by how you choose..." He thought about what he needed to do so he could handle this. His mother would run away. The Eric would not. His grandfather and his grandmother would not. He looked at the Triceratops and it, blemishes and all, looked back. There was no greatness, no absolute perfection; this was survival.

He smiled as he remembered Sarah trying to learn the word resolute, "How resoluted you are," she had said. Could he step up? Could he keep on? Right now he wanted to complain; he wanted to whine and throw things and run away. Could he resolve to struggle and struggle some more?

What if I do step up? Right now, he thought, inside Grandma's house, they are having to deal with Grandpa's body and funeral arrangements and truly adult stuff. *How could I help there?*

He could not, he decided. So, what could he do? He found two pressing things. The first? He had a one-hundred-word paper to write for school. *How can I pack my Grandpa into one-hundred words?*

The second? He had a carving to finish, sand, and varnish. It was still a memorial. It was still a reminder of two great men, and it was becoming something he was seeing, with his own eyes, as a possible future. *What if?* He calmed himself by breathing in and out, in rhythm with his own heart.

Before he did either of those things, he knew he had to do one more. He stood, picked up his dinosaur, and walked into the house. There, without so much as a word, he walked to his mother and gave her a big hug.

She was tongue-tied. *For once! That's as good as any Thanksgiving Day turkey.* Then: *Don't be snide. Let it happen.* He felt good even though he felt bad.

Scott moved to his grandmother who was seated on the couch, ragged with exhaustion. "Grandma," said Scott," I love you, and I loved your husband. Thank you for all you have done for me." He added, "For Mom and me."

"Darn you, Scott," she said, as tears began to well

again, "I've done enough crying today!" The smile on her face showed she had not lost her sense of humor, and he smiled too. They squeezed each other's hands, and he realized a third thing he needed to do. When was the last time he had made cookies for her?

Scott retraced his steps to the shop, once his grandfather's and now Scott's second home. He opened the laptop to work on the one-hundred words. He began: "Stanley Scott Schyler spoke not..." He stopped. Grandpa's third recommendation was to prepare. Scott looked around the room. He breathed deeply, in through his nose, out through his mouth. He did this five times and then did it again. He smelled the cedar. He looked at the carvings and tools, and he knew he could... *Thank you, Grandpa!*

He was following a plan. He began to type again. *One Hundred Words is Not Enough, by Slim Scott Stanley Schyler.* He kept the *Slim*. Twenty minutes later, he had a rough draft. He set it aside, expecting to read and edit it later.

He moved to his carving, now sketched, on the cherry and maple block. The roundish sort of Valentine was more of a mass, an ovoid egg-shape, with a slight V at the top. He wished his heart to be authentic, so he had also penciled in all the tubes. These were the inferior vena cava, the left pulmonary artery, and others. There was also a tricky one called the aortic arch. It looked to Scott like it was separate and flowing over the tube called the pulmonary trunk. He would have to go slow on that one. When he was done, he hoped it would look like a cool piece of art, but that it would also be close to the real thing.

He thoughtfully pulled the carving knife from its sheath and touched his father's initials. He sharpened his knife as both men had taught him, oiling the whetstone and angling the blade just right. He breathed again and thought about the individuals for whom he was creating. One he had barely known; the other had taught him much more than just carving.

He also whittled his heart for the two women that had given their hearts to their husbands. He could not fully understand that commitment yet, but his opening up to Sarah was maybe a small part of what true love looked like.

As he carved, he also thought about where this new vision of an amazing part of the human body might take him. Obviously, it was a concern. What if he paid more attention in science? What if he learned to work on the real thing?

Slim Scott Schyler got to work. Here was his Thanksgiving Day. He trimmed and scraped, cut, and sanded. He whistled "She'll Be Comin' 'Round the Mountain."

His plan was to have the heart and the plaque completed by the funeral on Monday. He had three more days. As he worked, he also made sure, for his grandmother, that he kept all his fingers.

17 | Taps

THE ROUTE 7–B SCHOOL BUS had just passed Grandma Ray's house on what should have been his third day of school, and he was not in it. *Really? Why couldn't it pass by my house?* It was only Grandma's now, even though Grandpa would always be there in the works he had created and the love and lessons he had offered.

Scott sat on the front steps eating one of the cherry-chocolate-fudge bars his grandmother liked so much. He had made these yesterday, with the help of his mother. Unbelievably, this task had brought them together. They had laughed and talked about Dad and Grandpa. They even talked about her parents, and how they had died so early. She had told him she still got angry about not knowing them. She could understand very much how he felt. *Who knew we could hold a conversation?*

They had not fought once, well, except for Scott's wanting to add more chocolate chips. They agreed that Grandma Ray should be recognized for all she had done for Grandpa and for Scott (and Addison), not just milk and cookies and antiseptic and bandages but for hugs and inspiration and comfort and love... These last three things were intangibles, impossible to carve or recreate in physical form, but without them, you have no heart!

His mother, also munching a fudge bar, sat with him on the porch in the spot where Moses usually perched. The giant bird had been moved to the grave site to greet the mourners.

"Are you ready?" Scott's mom asked. "The limo will be here in twenty minutes."

"I will be, Mom. I need to go get stuff from the shop." Nobody corrected his usage of stuff. He stood up and brushed the crumbs off his dark blue suit jacket and his T-Rex tie. That had been a gift from his grandparents. He looked down at his newly polished Frankenshoes. *Not so awkward in the right place at the right time.*

"Great job on these cookies, Honeybunch. Whoops, Scott."

"Mom, it's okay. You can call me that if you want, just not in the middle of school!"

"Gotcha!" She smiled. The pressure and anger between them was easing. They had spent a good amount of time learning from each other the last few days. *Death seems to give people time and reason to think,* thought Scott.

"Scott," she added as he turned to walk away, "Thanks for talking to me. You're a good son."

"You too, Mom."

Scott took off for the garage. He opened the door, flicked on the lights, and he remembered Grandpa again through the aromas of cedar, oak, spruce, and maple. Scott inhaled deeply.

He crossed to the bench and opened the laptop. Reading *One-Hundred Words* one more time, he thought Miss Walters might like what he had written. He hoped everyone else would. Then, he read it out loud for practice. His words boomed through the expanse of the shop, and the wooden otter, nearly finished but not touched for some time, seemed to wink at him. *Can I finish that for you, Grandpa?* He made sure the eulogy had saved and felt inside his suit pocket to see if the printed copy was there too. It was.

Next to the laptop was the pair of mini drumsticks, carved by his grandfather and given to him by Grandma Ray when he was younger and beating his head against... everything. He reached for them fondly and placed them in his right-side pocket. In the left pocket was a nesting and newly repaired Triceratops. Scott patted it for luck.

Scott found he was carrying more things to a funeral than he had taken to Tennessee. He unwrapped The Schyler Heart from a protective towel. It still smelled of drying shellac. He admired it, thinking that Grandpa Stanley would have been proud. *It's even better than I expected!* He answered, *That's not sayin' much!* Then: *Stop it!*

He had to admit it looked cool. The spalted maple showed the veining of the marbleized part of the heart while the cherry provided the warmth via the deep reds. Under the heart was a plaque, also made of cherry, that served as the base. He had made it too large, wanting to wood-burn the one-hundred words on it, but that had not worked... *A mistake is learning too. I still hate that!* But, instead of throwing it all against the wall, he had breathed, gotten a new piece, and started again. He had shortened the message to read:

Stanley Scott Schyler, Senior
Stanley Scott Schyler, Junior

Two Husbands • Two Fathers • One Grandfather
Both Teachers

With hearts beating in love for all.

Stanley Scott Schyler's grandson smiled at the completed project, rewrapped it in the towel, and placed it in a shopping bag. Already in the bag was his pair of S.S.S.S. identified drumsticks. He grinned. The fourth S could stand for Sarah. He could carve an &. "Whoa!" he said out loud. "Way too ahead of yourself!" *How about just a second hug?*

"Scott?" His mom called from the back door. "The limo's here."

"Coming, Mom," he replied. He picked up the bag and took one last look around to make sure he had everything. "Let's see," he said, "cookies, check; plaque and heart, check; drumsticks… and drumsticks, check; *One-hundred words*, check." He reached down to the floor and picked up his snare drum and the marching strap. "Now, I am ready," he said. "Love you, Grandpa." He turned off the light and closed the door.

Grandma Ray met Scott in the kitchen; his mother stood beside her. Both were teary-eyed again, normal for the occasion. Setting his bag and drum on the kitchen counter, he hugged his grandmother for what must have been the eightieth time that weekend. She needed them. He needed them.

"Are you all set?" she asked. Scott had asked her if he could be involved in the funeral. Once he had explained what he had in mind, his mom had asked, "Are you sure you can handle all that?" Scott had scowled, and then he promised he would not let either of them down.

"Yes. I am," he said, sounding more confident than he felt. His stomach was in knots, but he had been learning how to better deal with who he was.

"Grandma, could you sit down a minute? I want to give you something."

"We've got to go, Scott. The limo guys are waiting." Mom's impatience was churning.

"It's okay, Mom. It'll only take a minute." *Grandpa's gonna stay dead!* Then: *Too harsh!*

Scott grabbed the bag and guided Grandma to the living room sofa where they both sat down.

"It's not the greatest wrapping job but..." Scott pulled the towel-covered carving from the bag, held the base, and began to uncover the sculpture.

His grandmother peered at the checkerboard heart in Scott's hand. It almost seemed to beat. "Let your subject come alive," his grandpa had said.

Grandma Ray was not sure what to say; his mother's reaction was the same. It was hard to read their expressions.

"Scott…" Grandma Ray tried to speak, but she began to cry instead. "Oh, Scott…"

Addison read the inscription aloud, finishing with, "…love for all." She also started to weep.

"But don't you like it?" Scott's carving had had some effect, but was it the right one? Had he tried too hard to fill his grandfather's carving shoes?

He stood and stepped away. He felt too tall, too awkward, and he relapsed into another bout of Frankenshoes inferiority. *What a stupid idea!* He began to wrap it back up.

His mother spoke first. "Don't you dare! Scott, that is amazing." *It's only you saying that, Mom!*

His grandmother stood and took the heart from him. She turned it around, viewed it from all sides and then took her time reading the inscription, wiping her eyes all the while.

Without speaking, she walked to the front of the living room. A table had been set up that overflowed with flowers and cards from relatives, friends, and business acquaintances. There were even cards, arrangements, and wreathes on the floor. Obviously, Grandpa Stanley had been admired and loved. The Methodist church had sent over a large arrangement of lilies and roses that Grandma had used as a center piece. She moved it to one side.

Gently she placed Scott's heart—her son's heart, her husband's heart—front and center. She turned back to Scott and said maybe the best thing he would ever hear. "You have a lot of your grandfather in you."

Then, she grabbed his hands and started to count: "One, two, three, four, five..."

Scott was confused. "What are you doing, Grandma?"

She moved to the second hand. "...Six, seven, eight, nine, ten." She grinned. "Good, they're all still there!" They all shared a laugh. "Now," said Grandma Ray, "let's go get this thing done."

THE SERVICE FOR GRANDPA Stanley was standing room only at the Methodist church. *So many! Why do they only show up when you die?*

The limo ride was not all it was cracked up to be, mostly because the ride had only been for three blocks, but they would use it later to go to the cemetery. During the service, the pastor spoke of friends and family and how Grandpa would live on in our hearts...

Scott also had asked to speak, which is what had bothered his mother. Perhaps what she did not remember were all the times, as far back as *L'Orange*, where she had taught him to speak up, to be clear. Both his parents and grandparents had taught him to be professional. He would do his best.

The pastor introduced him. Scott walked to the podium, his heart nervously fluttering every Frankenstep of the way, but, he thought, it was not a bad flutter. He had something to tell whoever would listen about the coolest person he had ever met. He scanned the room, smiled at his mom and grandmother, took one final deep breath, and he began. Here is what a grandson said about his grandfather, in exactly one hundred words:

ONE HUNDRED WORDS IS NOT ENOUGH
by
Slim Scott Stanley Schyler

Stanley Scott Schyler spoke not just to hear himself speak.

He loved his wife of forty years not as an obligation or to take advantage.

He did not create, through wood and chisel, items that would prove his importance to others.

Stanley Scott Schyler, my grandfather, of strong hands and good heart, created to let the subject live through him.

He loved, without condition, even those others might consider unlovable.

He spoke to teach, passing on years of wisdom to empower others,

to create for themselves a better, stronger, and happier life than his had been.

Thank you, Grandpa Stanley!

He spoke clearly and well, with only a couple of gurgly pauses for teary reminiscences, then he sat down. He did not hear, nor did he want, applause. Today was not the day to say, "I am here." He only sought to show the spirit and life of his best friend.

There came the benediction, after which he had to stand in the procession line at the back of the church before leaving for the cemetery. He was hot, and he didn't know anyone. Like his grandmother, he wanted to get this over with.

He was startled to see Miss Walters in line. *How in the world?* He shook her hand and introduced her. "Mom, Grandma, this is my English teacher, Miss Walters."

Grandma Ray said, "I know. She told me last Sunday."

"I've been attending here for years, Scott." She turned square to face him. "Did you write that?"

"Oh, up there?" Scott nodded toward the church front. "Well, yeah."

"That was exemplary. You showed us who Stanley was. You painted a picture through your writing."

Scott didn't want to be graded in church. "So, like, is that an A plus?" His sarcasm bled through his suit coat.

Miss Walters heard his disappointment. "Scott, I told you the other day I thought your writing would be good. It's not about a grade. I'm sorry if I made it sound like that; that's the teacher in me. It's about life. You made your grandfather come alive to us!"

"Oh." He could do no better at this moment. "Thanks."

"You're welcome. I'll see you in class tomorrow." She turned to Addison. "Nice meeting you, Mrs. Schyler. That boy has quite a talent."

Mother and son beamed.

Slim Scott Stanley Schyler had prepared one more step in the Stanley Scott Schyler Senior tribute. It would happen at the Englewood Cemetery six miles away, and Scott worried he could make it happen. He would need some help and he hated asking for it. He had forced himself to answer another *What if?*

Now, peering out the limo window, he saw what he had hoped to see, and his heart leapt. A bent blue Subaru was parked along the route. Standing beside it were two people he did know: Sarah and The Eric. *This might work!*

The limousine drove through the gates of the cemetery and stopped about two hundred yards from the actual grave site. Scott climbed out of the car, taking with him his snare and sticks. He helped his grandmother and mother get out, kissed them, and left them. The two women moved to the front of the hearse where they waited for Scott to re-join them.

The plan was to lead the hearse and walk the final way through the elms, the oaks, and the pines that Stanley had loved so much. Once there, they would be greeted by a grand golden eagle named Moses, his mighty wings spread in welcome.

The Eric and Sarah met Scott at the hearse. The Eric also carried his snare, sticks, and marching strap. They all said, "Hi," then Sarah left the boys to join the other two women in front of the vehicle. As she walked away, she smiled and said, "Good luck."

He smiled back. "Thank you."

Scott had originally thought he would do this next step—lead the procession—alone. He was finding other people were a little okay; you just had to learn to trust the right ones. He had bravely asked The Eric to join him. The Eric had, thankfully, said yes.

When The Eric had told him that Sarah wanted to attend as well, part of Scott was still not sure whether it was because she liked him, or that she just wanted to get out of school. *Cynic!* Either way, he was happy she was there.

As mourners gathered at the grave, both boys attached harness to their snare drums and checked their sticks. The two percussionists took their positions about ten feet ahead of the ladies. Scott raised his sticks to form an X; The Eric did the same.

The drummers had worked out a pattern—solemn and fitting. Taps on a drum would replace taps from a bugle. Scott rapped his sticks together and quietly counted, "One, two, three, four." He placed his left Frankenshoe in front of his right while The Eric matched his steps.

They had planned a progression of the Single Drag Tap. Scott would play, go silent, and The Eric would play. It was an uncomplicated cadence: One, two and three; One, two and three... The pace was slow—about sixty beats per minute—the beat of a human heart. As they traded off, the beat was precise, clear, and calm;

the sounds echoed through the trees around them and was music and life to Scott's soul. In this way, the two led the procession.

As they walked, Scott considered the words of a man named Koestenbaum, who had discovered what Scott was trying to learn: "Greatness comes by your attitude." He was, he hoped, beginning to get it. Greatness does not need to be a grand show. Greatness is not always about being noticed. It is about learning who you are and holding onto that for all you are worth. It can be as simple as one small tap on one small drum by a fourteen-year-old boy who is learning he is more than mediocre, with the help of a friend.

Scott counted the duo to a stop: "One, two, ready, halt," Scott turned to The Eric and said, "Thank you."

Eric replied, "Glad to."

Drums set aside, and with Moses looking on, all was quiet as the pastor said a final prayer.

Scott had one more task. On the casket lid, he lovingly placed his original toy drumsticks, the first things ever carved for him. Scott whispered, "Thank you, Grandpa Stanley. Carve me something grand." He took hold of the hands of his mother and grandmother.

"Let's eat," said Grandma Ray, which is what they did.

TUESDAY MORNING ARRIVED and along with it came the real world. *Can it be much realer than death?* Scott knew he would still have to deal with the Steve Martins and the Mr. Ogden's of the world. He knew he would not always be *Mr. Happy*. He knew there were times when he would still like to throw things.

He also felt stronger than he ever had. "Greatness comes by how resolute you are," Scott was learning. *What will I do next?* He was reasonably sure it would include a muscle of the human body. He was also and ever curious about how life happens to you, but he was also considering how you can happen to life and to those around you. He thought of Ariel and Rodney, of Steve Martin, of Amanda and the *L'Orange* team. And his mom. *We all wish to be noticed! Does considering about how others act and react as they strive to survive help us talk to each other?*

He thought of The Eric and his Grandfather, good listeners both. He might experiment. His first subject? Mr. Ogden. *If I can drum major for that guy... Then: Be nice.*

As he walked the two blocks to his bus stop, he was hoping that Sarah might have missed him. After the service, he had not had the chance to see her; they had texted only briefly.

The bus squeaked its brakes to a stop; the door swung open, and Slim Scott Schyler climbed aboard.

He looked to his left and found Darla and Sarah. As he passed, Sarah grabbed his hand. "I'm sorry," she said.

"Thanks," he replied. He gripped her hand for longer than was *professional*. She didn't seem to mind. He turned toward Matthew who was eating a banana and clearing Scott's seat of the peel. "What? No cube?" Scott asked.

"No, my grades suck so Mom took it away."

Scott said, "There's more to life." He reached into his bag and pulled out his Triceratops. "Do you like dinosaurs?" he asked.

Matthew said, "Yeah" and took it from Scott. "What's its name?"

"Stanley," said Scott, as the bus pulled away in a cloud of fumes.

Acknowledgements

THIS TALE OF THE HEART began in 1993 as a short story, submitted to a contest and returned with the admonition that I should create a children's novel. Years later, after grown children and personal growth, I have attempted exactly that. I have twenty years' worth of middle and high school students to thank for having been my guinea pigs as I observed and learned from them, and really, they are who this book is for.

It was during that time that I met a man named Pete Koestenbaum (in Reader's Digest) and his view of greatness. He may not be aware of how many people he touched with that message, but it changed my life.

I have two of my own children, Darcy and Jeffrey, to thank for putting up with their dad's incessant retelling of woeful stories. I want to also thank Brendan King for his assistance on the cover design. I thank my mother-in-law Karen and her husband Bob—she for editing, and he for appreciating the content. The idea that they read the entire book aloud together is something I would wish more families to do with more books than just mine. I thank my cousin Linda who was first to read the roughest of drafts with glee and tears (hopefully at the appropriate times). Finally, I thank my wife Tamara for her patience as I continue to search for my own greatness in a myriad of forms. Ya'll are loved!

ABOUT THE AUTHOR

KENN BORDEN IS A jack of many trades: carpentry, radio, sales, and education. He is also a parent and husband. In each case, he has taught what he has learned, and he continues to practice, as he knows he has not yet mastered. Kenn is a writer of over 1000 radio commercials, a screenplay, short stories and many a silly poem. He lives in Brighton, Colorado with his wife, Tamara. To talk books, and to order books, please contact Kenn at: tutorman9@gmail.com

www.ingramcontent.com/pod-product-compliance
Lightning Source LLC
Chambersburg PA
CBHW021320190726
48288CB00003B/901